MAUREEN CHILD

is a California native who loves to travel. Every chance they get, she and her husband are taking off on another research trip. The author of more than sixty books, Maureen loves a happy ending and still swears that she has the best job in the world. She lives in Southern California with her husband, two children and a golden retriever with delusions of grandeur. Visit Maureen's website at www.maureenchild.com.

SANDRA HYATT

After completing a business degree, traveling and then settling into a career in marketing, Sandra Hyatt was relieved to experience one of life's eureka moments while on maternity leave—she discovered that writing books, although a lot slower, was just as much fun as reading them.

She knows life doesn't always hand out happy endings and figures that's why books ought to. She loves being along for the journey with her characters as they work around, over and through the obstacles standing in their way.

Sandra has lived in both the U.S. and England and currently lives near the coast in New Zealand with her high-school sweetheart and their two children.

You can visit her at www.sandrahyatt.com.

MAUREEN CHILD
&
SANDRA HYATT

UNDER THE MILLIONAIRE'S MISTLETOE

Silhouette ®

Desire

Published by Silhouette Books

America's Publisher of Contemporary Romance

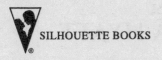 SILHOUETTE BOOKS

ISBN-13: 978-0-373-73069-8

UNDER THE MILLIONAIRE'S MISTLETOE

Recycling programs for this product may not exist in your area.

Copyright © 2010 by Harlequin Books S.A.

The publisher acknowledges the copyright holders of the individual works as follows:

THE WRONG BROTHER
Copyright © 2010 by Maureen Child

MISTLETOE MAGIC
Copyright © 2010 by Sandra Hyatt

CONTENTS

Dear Reader,

Holiday parties, snowball fights, kisses under the mistletoe…Christmas really *is* the most wonderful time of the year, just as the song promises! This month, *USA TODAY* bestselling authors Maureen Child and Sandra Hyatt reveal what happens *Under the Millionaire's Mistletoe* in two novellas.

Enjoy this powerful, passionate and provocative read!

Krista Stroever

Senior Editor

THE WRONG BROTHER

MAUREEN CHILD

For my mom, Sallye Carberry,
who loves Christmas more than anyone else I know.
You always made the magic for us, Mom.

One

Anna Cameron ducked behind a tinsel-draped potted plant and peeked through the lacy fronds at the mingling crowd. The Cameron Leather company Christmas party was in high gear. People she'd known most of her life were here, laughing, talking, drinking. She wished she were out there in the middle of them enjoying herself.

Instead, she was hiding from her stepmother. Not that Clarissa Cameron was an evil woman or anything. But she'd had a little too much to drink and now all she wanted to do was corner Anna and try to convince her to win back her former boyfriend, Garret Hale.

"As if I'd take him back," Anna muttered, pulling aside a tinsel-decorated frond to scan the crowd in front of her.

They'd gone out only a few times when Garret's older brother Samuel told him to drop her. He'd actually had the nerve to suggest that Anna was doing exactly what

Clarissa now *wanted* her to do. Using Garret to help her father's company. Okay, fine, a merger with Hale Luxury Autos would probably save Cameron Leather, but she wasn't a bargaining chip. And even if she had been, it wouldn't have worked.

Because Garret had backed away from her so fast that he'd left sparks in his wake. He hadn't stood up for her to his snooty, suspicious older brother. He'd called Anna to tell her they couldn't see each other anymore because the Great Sam Hale had decreed it. He'd threatened to cut Garret off financially if he hadn't stopped seeing Anna.

"No loss," Anna reassured herself. So despite what Clarissa wanted, Anna wouldn't have Garret back on a platter. She hadn't even been that interested in the man in the first place. One kiss had told her everything she needed to know about him. She hadn't felt the slightest tingle of expectation when he kissed her. Hadn't seen a single star. She had known then that he was not the man for her.

She wanted the *magic*.

Of course, the fact that he'd wimped out for the sake of his big brother and his wallet didn't exactly endear him to her either. And her life might have been easier if she could just admit to Clarissa what had happened. But she had a *little* pride after all.

Clarissa kept urging her to do exactly what Garret's brother had assumed she was up to in the first place— marry the man and bring a nice merger to the family business.

"Anna, honey, is that you in there?"

She jerked, startled and turned to look guiltily into her father's eyes. "Um, hi, Dad."

"What're you doing behind a plant, sweetie?" Dave

Cameron's green eyes were smiling, but Anna couldn't help but notice that there was a glimmer of worry there, too.

How to explain that she was hiding from his wife? Nope, couldn't do it. It wasn't anyone's fault, but Clarissa and Anna had never been as close as her dad wanted them to be. Until ten years ago, it had been just her and her father. Her own mother had died when Anna was two, so all she really had were photographs and her dad's stories.

When Clarissa came into their lives, Anna was seventeen. She hadn't been interested in acquiring a new "mother," and at the time had really resented having to share her father's affections. She and Clarissa had finally gotten to the point where they could be friends, if not mother and daughter, but Anna knew her father still worried about their relationship.

So, instead of blurting out the truth, Anna ran her fingertips across the top of the big blue ceramic pot. "Just checking to make sure everything's tidy. Yep, no dust."

He laughed and took her arm, drawing her out from behind the palm. "Housekeeping has never been one of your interests, so what's really going on?"

The music was too loud for any deep conversation and Anna wasn't interested in having one anyway. So she simply smiled, kissed her father's cheek and said, "Nothing, Dad. Everything's great. The party's wonderful."

"So wonderful you're hiding in the shrubbery?"

"Honestly?" she said, mentally crossing her fingers for the tiny lie she was about to tell, "Darren Shivers has had one beer too many and wanted to tell me all about how he won the high school football game back in the seventies."

"Oh, he's not telling that story again, is he?"

"You know Darren," she said, telling herself that really, it wasn't much of a lie. Any time the man had more than three beers, he cornered someone and forced him or her to relive his glory days with him. Still, couldn't hurt to change the subject. "Looks like everyone's having fun."

"Seem to be," he mused, swiftly scanning the crowd that was even now dancing to the music and gathering in knots to try to talk. "Your stepmother's done a fine job."

"Yes, Clarissa's very good at this sort of thing," she said, meaning it. She and her stepmother did have common ground after all. They both loved Anna's dad.

Her dad sent her a sidelong glance. "Is there something going on between you two?"

"Absolutely not," she said, unwilling to put her father in the middle of all this. Besides, Anna knew that Clarissa's tipsy attempt at matchmaking was only because she was worried about her husband.

Hard to fault her for that when Anna was worried, too.

Cameron Leather company was in trouble and despite this wonderful party, the truth was, if something great didn't happen soon, her dad was going to lose the company he'd built up from nothing. But Dave Cameron was an "old school" kind of man. He treated the women in his life like princesses and didn't want them "fretting" about company concerns. Her dad was sweet and old-fashioned and she loved him fiercely.

She forced a smile on to her face and said, "Don't worry about Clarissa and me. We're fine. And it's a great party, Dad. Why don't you go enjoy it?"

"Good idea." He took a step, stopped and asked,

"You're not going back behind that plant are you? You're too beautiful to hide away."

She held up one hand. "I swear. I will have a good time. Now go, dance with your wife."

And keep her off my trail, she added silently.

By the time her father had slipped back into the crowd, greeting old friends with a forced holiday cheer, Anna had disappeared from the ballroom. As a child, she'd explored every inch of the big house, so she knew all the nooks and crannies to disappear into.

She was stopped a dozen times to talk to someone or answer a question from the catering staff. The music jumped into a wild dance beat with a tune from the forties and the drumbeats seemed to echo in the headache behind her eyes.

"Clarissa's looking for you," someone said and Anna smiled and kept moving. *Just nod,* she told herself. Smile and keep walking.

She was almost at the long hallway leading to the front door when she heard, "Anna!"

She stopped again with a barely restrained sigh. Not an easy thing to do at all, she thought, slipping out of a party where she knew everyone. She turned to chat yet again with one of her father's employees.

Eddie Hanover was short, round and sported a wispy gray comb-over. He was one of the guys Anna had grown up around and she loved him like a second father. "Hi, Eddie. How's it going?"

"Going great, Anna. Trust your dad to hold to traditions even when times are hard," he said with a grin.

True. Her father hadn't wanted to even discuss canceling the annual Christmas party. The company might be in trouble, but her dad wouldn't "cheat" his employees out of something they looked forward to all year.

"Have you seen Clarissa?" Eddie's wife Trina asked. "She's been looking all over for you."

"Well, I'll go look for her." In the driveway. Inside her own car.

"Just wanted to say howdy, let you know we all appreciate the Camerons throwing the party," Eddie told her, then grabbed Trina's hand and dragged her off in the direction of the music.

She nodded, but the pair were already lost in the mingling crowd. Then she caught a flash of something bright red out of the corner of her eye. When she glanced over, she saw it was Clarissa, headed her way.

Think fast, she told herself. If only she were dating someone else, she thought frantically. Then Clarissa would have to give up on the whole "marry for the sake of the family" idea and she'd drop the subject of Garret Hale for good.

Unfortunately, there was no man in Anna's life and no prospects for one anytime soon. Her gaze scanning the room, frantically trying to find an escape route, she eventually spotted something even better.

A tall man with no woman clinging to his arm, standing beneath a red ribbon–bedecked sprig of mistletoe.

With Clarissa hot on her heels, Anna sprinted toward him, moving in and out of the ever-shifting crowd like a race car driver on a complicated course. When she was right behind him, she tapped him on the shoulder and shouted to be heard over the pounding music.

"Kiss me and save my life!"

Two

He spun around, his lake-blue eyes fixed on her. Then he smiled, reached for her and said, "My pleasure."

She barely had time to take a breath before his mouth came down on hers. He wrapped his arms around her, held her tight and kissed her as she'd never been kissed before. Long and hard and deep, he sent sparks of something wonderful shooting through her system. His tongue tangled with hers as he tasted her completely and Anna found herself melting into him, giving herself up to the incredible glory of what he was making her feel.

The magic she used to dream about was here. Finally here. In the arms of a man she'd never met before.

Who was her newfound hero anyway?

"Oh, Anna!"

Clarissa's voice penetrated the lovely glow surrounding her and Anna reluctantly broke the kiss, pulling back just enough to stare up into her rescuer's blue eyes.

Really, the man was drop-dead gorgeous. No, better. He was bring-the-dead-back-to-life gorgeous. Lake-blue eyes, night-black hair, a strong jaw and shoulders wide enough to belong to a professional football player.

The music was playing, the steady roar of conversations continued to roll on, but she felt as though she and her mystery man were all alone in the world. Until Clarissa piped up again.

"You should have told me!"

"What?" she asked, still looking into those deep blue eyes. "Told you what?"

Clarissa moved in close, gave Anna a tight hug and said, "You should have told me that the reason you stopped seeing Garret was because you were involved with his *brother!*"

Brother?

"*You're* Anna Cameron?"

"*You're* Sam Hale?"

"This is *wonderful,*" Clarissa said on a satisfied sigh.

This was a nightmare, Sam Hale told himself, looking down at the pretty woman who had just knocked his socks off.

He didn't belong there and he knew it. Didn't matter that he'd been invited to the Cameron Christmas party. Hell, it looked as if half of Crystal Bay, California, was crammed into the ballroom of Dave Cameron's big house on the sea.

But he wasn't there for the warm holiday celebration, he'd come to get an up close look at Dave's daughter. Of course he'd seen pictures of her, but he hadn't had the time to recognize her before that mind-numbing kiss. The woman he'd heard so much about from his brother,

Garret. The same woman who was now looking at him as if he'd just crawled out from under a rock.

He was here to find out if maybe he'd been wrong about the woman. It was no secret that Cameron Leather was in trouble. And the fact that Dave Cameron's daughter had been dating *his* brother had just seemed too coincidental to Sam. He'd figured that some wily, sneaky, money-hungry woman had latched on to Garret for one reason only.

Cash.

But Garret was still pissed about this, so Sam had decided to see for himself if his suspicions were true. If he was wrong about her, he could try to smooth things over between this woman and his brother.

He was off to a hell of a start.

"I can't believe you kissed me!" she accused.

"You asked me to," he reminded her. And there was nothing he'd like better at the moment than to kiss her again. As soon as that thought hit his brain, his blood started humming. He was ready and willing and all too damn eager to give in to his desires. So, he clung to the threads of his anger and used them to fight back the growing rush of want.

She pointed to the arched doorjamb above his head. "You're standing under mistletoe. And I didn't know it was *you,* now, did I?" the redhead with the beautiful eyes argued.

"Anna, you two shouldn't bicker," Clarissa lowered her voice and leaned in to make sure she was heard. "It's a party."

"This isn't what you think it is," Anna said, still glaring at him.

What he should do is leave. Distance himself from this

whole mess. But he couldn't quite make himself walk away from her. At least, not yet.

"Lovers' quarrels," the older woman said, "happens to everyone, dear."

"Oh, God," Anna whispered.

Then she licked her lips and Sam's insides tightened. His focus was narrowed on her. This woman was nothing like what he'd expected. The kind of woman his brother usually went for was—*less* than this one. This woman had fire inside her and a mind of her own. She clearly wasn't an empty-headed party girl looking for a good time. The question was, was she a mercenary woman looking for a fat wallet?

"I can't believe this," she muttered.

Damned if he'd stand there and be accused of being a lecher or something. "You know, I was just standing there minding my own business..."

"Have you met my husband?" Clarissa asked.

"You should have introduced yourself," Anna told him.

"Before or after you propositioned me?" he countered.

She gasped, outraged. "I did not!"

"You said, 'Kiss me and save my life,'" he reminded her with a grin. "What did you expect a man to do?"

"Okay, yes, I did. But I didn't know it was you."

"We covered that already," he said.

"I'll just find Dave," Clarissa said, tipsily oblivious. "He'll be so happy to know about the two of you!"

"Don't!" Anna spoke up quickly, but it was too late, the older woman was already disappearing into the crowd. "Oh, for heaven's sake."

"Now that we're alone, want to move back under the mistletoe?"

"No!" She flushed, though, and he knew she was lying. She stared helplessly after her stepmother for a long minute. Then whipping back around to glare at him again, she said, "You have to leave."

He'd been thinking the same damn thing a second ago. But now that she was practically ordering him out, Sam wasn't about to leave. "Hey, I was invited. Why should I leave just because you're suddenly regretting trying to seduce me?"

She hissed in a breath and her cheeks flamed with hot color. Amazing. He hadn't thought there were still women around who actually *blushed*. Sam was more intrigued by the minute—and even less inclined to leave than he had been.

"I did not try to seduce you," she said through gritted teeth. "It was a blip. An emergency situation."

He was starting to enjoy himself. "An emergency make out session?"

"We didn't—" She stopped, took a deep breath and closed her eyes briefly. "You know what? I'm not doing this anymore. If you're not going to leave, I will."

She turned around so fast that her long, auburn hair swung out behind her like a flag. She was wearing a sleeveless silver top that clung to her breasts and a short, black silk skirt that hugged her behind and defined every curve. Her long, lean legs looked as smooth and pale as fresh cream and the three-inch black heels she wore had a cutout at the toes that spotlighted dark red nails.

His gaze dropped to her behind as she hurried away from him and he had to admire the indignant sway of her hips. But damned if he was going to let her walk off and leave him standing there still buzzed from that kiss.

Sam caught up to her in a few long strides. Grabbing

her arm, he stopped her, then swung her around to face him.

She looked pointedly at his hand on her arm. "Excuse me?"

He laughed but let her go. "Does that snotty queen-to-peasant tone usually work on men?"

Her eyes widened. "I'm not the one who tells people how to live their lives," she told him flatly. "That would be *your* specialty, remember?"

A couple of guests wandered through the hallway and before he could suggest it, Anna pointed down the hall and he followed her. She was clearly looking for some privacy to finish this conversation. She led him to a pair of French doors that opened into a garden with a stone pathway laid out between the flower beds. She started off down the path and Sam was right behind her.

A glance to his left showed him bright lights spilling from the ballroom to lay across a wide, brick patio. The music was muted at a distance and the rush of people talking sounded like the sea, rising and falling in rhythm.

Only twenty or so feet away, it was as if he and Anna were alone in the world. There were no lights decorating this tidy garden, just the moonlight covering everything in a pale glow. She kept walking and Sam stayed close, until she stopped beside a stone bench encircling a small fountain in the shape of a dolphin.

The white noise of the falling water drowned out most of the party, but truth to tell, Sam was so caught up in the woman in front of him that he wouldn't have noticed a train blasting through the yard.

Satisfied that they were alone, Anna continued her rant as if she hadn't been interrupted.

"How is it you get to decide what people do and who they date?"

Irritated, he snapped, "I don't remember filling out your social calendar. As for my brother..."

"Did you or did you not tell him to stop dating me because I was—" She stopped and tapped her chin with the tip of one finger. "Let me see if I can get this just right. *She's using you to get to my money to save her father.*" She narrowed her eyes on him. "That about cover it?"

Hearing his own words tossed back at him caused him to wince. Figured that his brother would be fool enough to actually tell her what Sam had said. He should have known.

Most of his life, Sam had been taking care of Garret. He'd seen him through school, bailed him out of trouble occasionally and waited for him to grow up. Hadn't happened yet, though.

He moved in closer to her and had the satisfaction of seeing her eyes widen slightly at his nearness. Good to know he wasn't the only one still affected by that kiss.

"He shouldn't have repeated that to you."

"You shouldn't have said it in the first place."

"I'm looking out for my family."

"And what? I'm a threat?"

Looking at her now, Sam thought she was only a threat to a man's sanity. But how could he be sure she wasn't simply an excellent actress? If she was feigning insult, though, she was doing a damn good job of it.

"Babe, I don't know what you are. All I know is I do what I have to for my family—why shouldn't I expect you to do the same?"

"So you don't even deny saying it—and don't call me 'babe.'"

He scraped one hand across the back of his neck. "No, I don't. Can you deny that your father's company's in trouble?"

She took a deep breath and helplessly, Sam's gaze briefly dropped to the deep V of her shirt. When his eyes met hers again, he noted fresh fury sparking in her grass-green eyes.

Lowering her voice, she said, "Are you in the Middle Ages or something? You really believe I would *barter* myself to save my dad's company?"

"People have done a lot more for a lot less," he mused.

"Well, I don't," she told him. "And I really think you've insulted me enough for one night, don't you?"

"Yeah," he said, edging closer, "I think we've *both* done enough talking."

Staring down into her eyes, he reached for her and waited to see if she would pull away. She glared at him. He pulled her in closer, until her breasts were pillowed against his chest and he could feel the heat of her body sliding into his.

"This isn't a good idea," she said, tilting her head back to look up at him. "I should be kicking you."

"Yeah," he said, his gaze moving over her features as if trying to burn her image onto his brain. "But doesn't seem to matter. I've got to taste you again."

"Really not a good idea," she whispered, going up on her toes to meet him as he lowered his head to hers.

His lips brushed hers and he felt that zip of something amazing scatter through him. Her mouth opened under his and he swept inside, losing himself in her heat, her acceptance. He felt her heartbeat pounding against his chest and knew that his own heart was matching that wild rhythm.

She leaned into him and he swept her up, nearly lifting her off her feet to get her closer to him. He wanted more. Wanted bare skin beneath his hands. Wanted to ease her down on that damn bench and—

Close by, a raucous burst of laughter shattered the night as people started wandering out into the garden. The intrusion was enough to tear them apart instantly.

Sam took a step back from her, just for good measure, and he didn't think it was far enough. Her taste still filled his mouth and his blood was pumping through his veins as hot and thick as lava.

"This is crazy," she whispered, shaking her head as if she couldn't believe what was happening between them.

Sam knew exactly how she felt. "Doesn't seem to matter," he said, as he took a step closer to her.

An uneasy laugh shot from her throat. "We are not doing that again."

"Why not?" Yeah, he knew this was trouble. But he didn't really care.

"Because…" She mentally searched for a good reason and apparently came up empty. Still struggling for breath, she added, "We're just not going to, trust me. And if you won't leave, then I will."

She swept past him, chin lifted, head held high.

"Good night, Anna Cameron," he said softly.

She stopped, looked over her shoulder at him and said pointedly, "Good*bye,* Sam Hale."

Three

Sam didn't leave.

Instead, he wandered through the party, listening to snippets of conversation even as he tried to get her out of his mind. She wouldn't go, though. Instead, he kept seeing her eyes, filled with fury and dazzled with passion. He heard her voice, standing up to him as no one had dared do in years. She hadn't backed down. She'd stood her ground and challenged him. Argued with him.

And then kissed him senseless.

Why the hell had a woman like her ever dated Garret? he asked himself. She was way too much woman for his younger brother. Which led him back to his original thought, that she had only been dating Garret to try to help her father's company.

But if that were true, why wouldn't she have tried to snag *Sam?* Why not go for the head of the business?

He accepted a glass of wine from a passing waiter, had a sip, then set the flute down again on a nearby table. His gaze scanned the crowd, noting the decorations, the Christmas tree that had to stand ten feet tall and the mountain of small gifts beneath it, tokens for their guests, all wrapped in bright paper and festive ribbons.

Sam didn't know whether to admire Dave Cameron for going ahead with a party when times were so bad for his company, or to pity him for being a fool. The snippets of conversations he'd heard throughout the place told him that everyone in the room knew about Dave's troubles, so this party wasn't fooling anyone. Why do it, then?

"Having a good time?"

The voice behind him caught Sam off guard and his shoulders stiffened. He should have known that Dave Cameron would come and find him. Especially considering the man's wife had probably reported seeing Sam and Anna kissing like teenagers in the backseat of a car.

Turning, he held out his hand. "It's a good party, Dave."

"Glad you could come," the other man said, shaking his hand. "Don't recall seeing you here last year."

Or any other year. Sam didn't usually get involved in community activities. The only reason he was here this year was because he'd wanted a look at Anna. Now, he wanted another, longer look at her. "You know how it is," he said, "never enough time to relax."

"You should take the time," Dave told him. "There's more to life than business."

"So I hear."

The older man watched him thoughtfully. "Clarissa tells me you and Anna have...*met*."

Uncomfortable, Sam hedged. No doubt, the story of

that mistletoe kiss had already made the rounds, thanks to Clarissa. As it was, he felt the stares of at least a dozen people. Small towns were notorious for gossip, and Sam knew he and Anna were going to be the hot topic for at least a few days.

"Yeah. That's a long story, though," he said and gave a quick look around at the surrounding crowd. "Not really the time for it now."

Nodding, Dave said, "I'll look forward to hearing it."

"Right." Not a conversation Sam wanted to have. "Well, I only stopped by to wish you a Merry Christmas, so I think I'll be going."

"No need to rush off," Dave told him. "Stay, enjoy yourself."

The only way that would happen is if he could get Anna to himself again. And because the chance of that was slim, there was really no point in sticking around.

"I appreciate it. Another time." He took a step, then stopped and added, "Say good night to Anna for me."

Let her explain the situation to her father, he thought with an inner smile.

"Now that's a gorgeous Christmas tree."

Anna stepped back to admire her own handiwork and smiled at her best friend, Tula Barrons. Her real name was Tallulah, but heaven help you if you actually called her that. Tula's blond hair was cut short, close to her head. She wore silver hoop earrings, a blue tunic sweater and black jeans with navy blue boots.

"Thanks," Anna said. "I like a lot of lights."

"Yeah, they'll probably be able to spot that tree from space." Tula grinned as she carried in the lattes she'd gotten at the corner coffee bar.

Anna studied the tall Douglas fir. There were only four strands of a hundred lights on it. "Can you really overdo Christmas?" she wondered aloud. "I don't think so."

Tula handed her one of the lattes and took a long look at the tree herself. After a second or two, she nodded. "I think you're right."

"Plus, it looks great in the front window and maybe it'll draw in some holiday business." She could use it, Anna thought. Her shop, Faux Reality, had been all too quiet for the last couple of weeks.

But then, people weren't really thinking about faux finishes or trompe l'oeil paintings on their walls right now. They were too busy buying presents and baking. All good, she told herself, because Anna, too, loved the Christmas season. But she could do with a really big job about now, so she could go and do some Christmas shopping herself.

Tula took a sip of her latte and looked at Anna over the rim. "Is business that bad?"

Anna sighed. As a writer of children's books, Tula had her own worries, but at least she understood that making a career out of the "arts" was usually feast or famine. "Bad enough that I took a couple of quickie jobs painting storefront windows. Art is art, right? I mean, Christmas trees on windows is still painting."

"Absolutely." After taking another sip, Tula nodded and said, "So, I heard all about the big mistletoe *kiss* last night."

Anna choked on a gulp of hot latte. "You heard? How? Where?"

"Are you kidding?" Her friend laughed. "You've lived in Crystal Bay your whole life, just like me. You know the grapevine in town works faster than a Google search."

"Oh, God." Suddenly, the brightly lit tree wasn't uplifting her spirits quite so much anymore.

"Oh, yeah," Tula said, walking to the front counter and dropping onto one of the high-backed stools. "So spill. Tell me everything. Word is you and Sam Hale were lip-locked so completely that steam was lifting off the tops of your heads."

"Oh, this is perfect," Anna muttered.

"Sure sounded like it," Tula agreed, then asked, "still, I'm dying to know…wasn't it weird kissing the brother of the guy you used to go out with?"

Weird wasn't the word she'd use, Anna thought. Hot. Passionate. Intense. Crazy, even. All good words. Weird? Not so much.

"I really don't want to talk about this," she said, moving to hang one of her antique ornaments from a high branch of the tree.

"Nice attempt at evasion," Tula told her with a laugh. "But no way are you getting out of this. I left the party early, so I didn't see the show you two put on. But according to Kate, down at Espresso Heaven, people clear across the room from you guys were going up in flames."

"Just shoot me." Anna looked out the front window onto Main Street and imagined everyone in their shops taking about her. Just great.

"Come on, give a little," Tula whined. "I haven't had an actual date in six months and the least you could do is let a girl live vicariously."

"Just what I want to do."

"Was it great?"

"Are you going to let this go?"

Tula laughed. "Have you met me?"

Anna had to laugh, too. She and Tula had been best friends since junior high. They'd gone to college together and had planned to move to Paris and be famous. They never had made it to France, though, instead coming back to Crystal Bay. Anna had opened her own shop and Tula was making a name for herself as the author of the popular *Lonely Bunny* books.

Tula was loyal, a great friend and profoundly nosy. Anna knew darn well that her friend was never going to let this go.

"Fine," she said on a sigh. "It was incredible. Happy?"

"Not nearly. If it was so incredible, why do you look so bummed?"

Anna shook her head. "Hello? Don't you remember that Sam Hale is the guy who told his brother to dump me?"

Tula frowned and pointed out, "Yeah, and I remember that *Garret* Hale was the giant weasel dog who did the actual dumping."

"True." What kind of grown man took orders from his big brother? Anna wondered. But on the other hand, what kind of guy was Sam to step in and try to take over his younger brother's life?

"So, how'd you happen to bump into Sam's luscious mouth?"

Anna glared at her. "What makes you think it's luscious?"

"I'm not blind, you know. I have seen the man from a distance."

And one look would be enough for most women to curl up and whimper at his feet. Not that she was going to be doing any whimpering, thanks very much. "It was an accident."

"So you slipped and fell onto his mouth. Sure. As your

friend, I'm happy to buy that lame explanation." Tula took a sip of latte and leaned back against the counter. "The question is, why are you so touchy about it?"

"Because he was an ass and because I liked that kiss too much."

"Ah, that I get," Tula said, then straightened up, a look of horror on her face. "Oh, you never slept with Garret, did you?"

"Of course not!" Anna practically recoiled at the idea. The few kisses she'd shared with Garret hadn't exactly started a fire inside. "We only went out a few times."

"Good," Tula said with a chuckle, "because that could have been awkward. No guy wants to think you're comparing him to his own brother."

Remembering that long, amazing kiss under the mistletoe had Anna practically sighing. "Trust me when I say, there is no comparison."

"Aha!" Tula crowed. "You're all gooey-eyed and you just admitted that Sam's a better kisser than Garret. The plot thickens."

Anna laughed a little. Impossible to be mad at Tula, especially when she was right. "There is no plot. He still thinks I set out to deliberately trap his precious brother into marrying me so I could save Dad's company."

"Well, then, I don't care how great a kisser he is—he's an idiot."

"Thanks, pal," she said.

"You bet." Tula watched her for a second or two, then apparently decided a change of subject was needed. "I've got to drive down to Long Beach to see my cousin Sherry."

Since Crystal Bay was in northern California, going to Long Beach in the southern half of the state was at least a seven-hour drive.

"Why are you going? You guys aren't exactly close. Heck, it's been six years since you've seen her."

Tula shrugged and took another sip of her latte. "Yeah, but we're all the family either of us has…"

"You've always got me."

"I know," she said with a smile. "And thanks. But Sherry called and said she really needs to see me."

"And she can't come up here."

Wrinkling her nose, Tula said, "You know Sherry. Afraid of freeways, afraid of driving, afraid of flying… afraid, period. So I'm driving down today. Should be back in a few days. Want to have dinner when I get back?"

"Sure, just be safe and call if you need to. I know how Sherry gets to you."

Tula grinned. "I'm going to do a chant for patience all the way down the coast."

"Good idea," Anna said, realizing how grateful she was that Tula had stopped by this morning. Just being around her friend made her feel more herself. She'd spent most of the night before thinking about Sam Hale and those two amazing kisses. And she so didn't need to be thinking about him or his mouth, Anna told herself firmly.

She was back to normal—despite being the topic of gossip all over town.

She pushed that thought aside and tried to focus on work.

"Did you call that Mrs. Soren back?"

There had been a message on the answering machine when she arrived this morning. A woman wanted her to come out and give her an estimate on what it would cost to do a mural on her living room wall.

"Yep," Anna said. "I've got an appointment to see her

at one today. Fingers crossed it works out. Her house is on the bluff."

"Ooh," Tula said softly. "So it's probably one of those mansions like your dad's."

Anna nodded, but she knew all too well that a fabulous house didn't necessarily mean a lot of extra cash.

Her own father's house had been built more than thirty years ago. Looking at it, anyone would assume that the Cameron family's financial health was in great shape. Nothing could have been further from the truth. A twist of worry for her dad hit her hard and fast and for a second or two, she almost felt guilty for not falling in with Clarissa's plan to snag a rich husband.

Four

A few phone calls were all it took to give Sam all of the information he needed on Cameron Leather. Yes, the company was in trouble, but it wasn't in its death throes just yet. Dave Cameron had expanded when he should have been more cautious, but with a little judicious input of capital, the company would be back on its feet.

Didn't make him feel any better to realize that. All it told him was that the odds of Anna being exactly as mercenary as he suspected her to be just went a lot higher.

He leaned back in his desk chair and stared out the window at the backyard. Working from home had its perks. Even though Hale Luxury Autos had a full-size shop on the outskirts of town, Sam also had a specially built garage here at home. At the shop, his master mechanics, artists and upholsterers had free rein and he rarely stepped in. Here, he had his own setup and indulged himself whenever he felt the need to get his hands dirty.

His gaze fixed on the manicured lawn and garden that ran down a slope to the ocean below. Sam took a minute to realize just how far he'd come. He'd started out small, building custom cars for people with more money than taste.

Now, Sam had people flocking to him for his expertise and he spent most of his time trying to rein in the near-constant stream of paperwork involved.

"Mr. Hale?"

"Yes, Jenny?" He turned when his housekeeper opened the door and called to him.

"I made the call. Ms. Cameron will be here at one."

He smiled. "Excellent. Thanks."

When she left again to go back to the main house, Sam let his smile widen as he imagined the look on Anna's face when she arrived to give Mrs. Soren an estimate, only to find out *he* was the one who had initiated the call. She wouldn't be happy, but Sam needed to know her. If only to prove to himself he'd been right to break up her and his brother.

Smiling to himself, Sam stepped out of the multi-bayed garage. He studied the view and let his mind wander to the green-eyed redhead whose memory was torturing him.

"The living room is this way."

Anna followed the fiftyish woman down a parquet hallway to an arched doorway that opened into a huge room. Clearly masculine, the decor was mostly big leather chairs, heavy tables and brightly colored rugs scattered across the inlaid wood floor. A stone fireplace took up most of one wall and floor-to-ceiling windows displayed a view of the wide front lawn.

A huge, beautifully decorated Christmas tree stood in one corner, with wrapped gifts beneath it. Which reminded Anna just how much she needed this job.

"It's lovely," she said, meaning it. But she couldn't help wondering, "This is your husband's lair, isn't it?" she asked with a smile.

"My husband?" The woman laughed and waved one hand. "Oh, my, no. My husband died twenty years ago. This is my employer's house."

She was the housekeeper? Anna frowned and looked around the room, as if searching for a hint to the owner's identity. When she found nothing, she said, "I'm sorry. I thought you wanted to talk to me about painting a mural in here."

"No," a deep, familiar voice said from behind her. "Mrs. Soren made the call, but I'm the one who wants to hire you."

Anna went completely still. A setup. And she'd walked right into it. Turning around slowly, she looked up into Sam's blue eyes and, keeping her voice cool, she said, "I'm sorry. There's been a mistake."

He scowled at her. Small consolation, she knew, but she was pleased that she'd disrupted whatever plan he'd concocted.

Shifting his gaze to the other woman in the room, he said, "That's all, Jenny. Thanks."

"Yes, sir," she answered and nodded at Anna as she left.

"You had her lie for you. That's just low."

"She didn't lie."

Anna tipped her head to one side and tapped the toe

of her boot against the floor. "So you want to hire me? Please."

His eyebrows arched high on his forehead. "Are you always this crabby with a prospective customer?"

"You're not a customer, prospective or otherwise," she said firmly and clutched her portfolio closer to her chest.

He walked into the room and Anna couldn't help but notice how at home he looked in faded black jeans and the dark red T-shirt that clung to his broad chest. His black work boots hardly made a sound as he walked across the deep blue and green rug to stand in front of her.

"Business that good, then?" he asked. "You can turn down customers?"

"In my shop, I can do what I like."

"True, but seems shortsighted to turn down a job just because you're embarrassed about kissing me."

"What?" Her eyes widened and her jaw dropped. "Are you delusional?"

He smirked. "You seem a little sensitive."

"I'm not sensitive. I'm insulted."

"Don't know why. It was a great kiss."

True. Damn it.

"Look," Anna said, clinging to every stray fiber of her dignity, "we're wasting each other's time here and even if you can afford it, I can't."

"You agreed to give me an estimate on a wall mural," he reminded her. "The least you can do is keep your word."

Anna glared at him and the dirty look she gave him had zero effect on the man. If anything, he looked supremely pleased with himself. Well, fine. She'd keep the appointment and then when she quoted him an outrageous price, he'd tell her no and she'd leave. All she had to do was take control of this situation.

"Fine, then," she said. "What did you have in mind?"

He gave her a wide smile that tugged at something deep inside her. The man was a walking hormone party. Anna gave herself a stern, if silent, talking-to. There would be no more kissing. No more flirting.

No *anything* with Sam Hale.

"Actually," he said, spreading his arms wide to encompass the room, "I'd prefer to hear your opinion. What kind of murals do you usually suggest?"

Anything would look fabulous in the opulent room, but Anna wouldn't give him the satisfaction of saying so. She gave a quick look around and fixed her gaze on the wide, empty space above the fireplace.

"A window and garden scene would look nice there."

"A *window?*"

"Trompe l'oeil," she told him patiently.

"Optical illusion?"

"You could call it that," she said and in spite of what she was feeling, she found herself warming to her theme. She loved faux finishing. Loved the trompe l'oeil murals that mimicked reality so completely, she'd once seen a man try to pick up a marble that had been painted onto a tabletop.

"A close translation of the French name means *trick the eye*. With the right artist, you can pretty much remodel your entire home without lifting a hammer."

"And you're the 'right' artist?"

"I'm really good," she said simply.

"I bet you are."

She flushed a little and hated herself for it. But she

would defy any woman in the world to remain completely cool and unruffled with *this* particular man focusing all of his attention on her.

He watched her. "Explain what you mean about the painting."

She didn't know what he was up to, but as long as she was there anyway, she couldn't resist talking about her favorite kind of work. "For instance, on that long wall over there, I could paint a set of French doors opening onto an English garden. It would look real enough to convince you that you could step outside and smell the flowers." She looked back at him. "Or I could give you an ocean scene complete with crashing waves and seabirds overhead. I could really, within reason, give you anything you wanted."

Oh, boy, that had come out a lot different than it sounded in her head. He must have been thinking the same thing, because something hot and wicked flashed in his eyes.

"And what do you charge for this amazing service?"

She cleared her throat, inhaled sharply and told herself that he didn't really care. He wasn't actually interested. So she gave him a price well above what she would normally charge for a mural.

He didn't even blink.

"I'll give you twice that if you can have it done before Christmas."

"Are you serious?" He couldn't be, she told herself. This was all part of some twisted game. He'd brought her here for his own purposes, whatever they were, and now he was dangling a great job in front of her like bait.

The hell of it was, it was working.

"Yes, I'm serious," he told her, and walked toward her with slow, measured steps.

"Why?" Anna stared up into his deep blue eyes and didn't flinch from the gleam of passion she saw shining at her. "Why would you hire me? Why would you offer so much money?"

"Does it matter?"

She wrestled with that question for a second or two. Her mind raced with arguments, pro and con. One part of her wanted to throw his offer in his face and march out the door, head held high. The other, more practical side of her was shrieking, *Are you crazy? Take the job!*

In a couple more silent seconds, she had already tallied up the bills she could pay if she took the job he offered. It had been a slow couple of months in the world of faux finishing and with this one job, she could cover her expenses for another two months. Not to mention the Christmas presents she could buy if she took this commission.

The downside was obvious.

She'd be spending a lot of time with a man who both infuriated and excited her. Who needed that kind of irritation on a daily basis? Not to mention the fact that her body tended to light up like a fireworks display whenever he was within three feet of her. That couldn't end well.

"So what'll it be?" he asked, a sly smile on his face as if he knew she was arguing with herself. "Stay or go?"

His satisfied expression told Anna that he was completely sure of himself. He thought he had her pegged. That she was just another woman ready to grab the money and run.

She should go. She knew it. She'd love to be able to look into his eyes and say, "No, you can't buy me." But as satisfying as that sounded, she knew she wasn't going to walk away.

She couldn't afford to.

"Fine," she muttered. "I'll take the job."

"Thought you might."

To keep from saying something she would no doubt regret, she bit her tongue. The man was more irritating than he was gorgeous, which was really saying something. She'd work for him, Anna told herself, but she wasn't going to let him insult her for her trouble either.

"Just so you know," she told him with a patient tone she was proud of, "I'm only taking this job because I really need the work. But so we're clear…I don't like you."

His eyebrows winged up. "And yet, you're staying. So money talks?"

Make that even *more* irritating than he was gorgeous. He'd already told his younger brother to dump her because he thought she was after his money. Now, he was no doubt convinced that he'd been right about her, which just made her furious.

"Easy to say money doesn't matter when you have plenty of it," she pointed out.

"Yeah, it is." Then he said, "Not the point of this, though. The point is, even though you hate me personally, you're more than willing to take my money."

"Less willing every second," she muttered.

"That I don't believe."

Anna narrowed her gaze on him and asked, "Are you trying to make me quit before I've even started?"

"Nope, just waiting to see how long you could hold on to your temper."

"Not much longer," she admitted. Taking a breath, she said, "If it's all right with you, I'll start tomorrow."

"Fine. I'll expect you at eight."

"Fine."

"Fine."

"Well," she said after a simmering few seconds, "this is childish."

"I'm sort of enjoying it."

"Color me surprised," she told him. "But believe it or not, some of us have other, more important things to do."

He grinned and Anna took a breath. Why was it *this* man who got to her so easily? Where was the indifference she'd felt for his brother? Why did the *wrong* brother feel so right?

If this was some sort of test of her morals, Anna thought, she was already failing badly. It was taking every ounce of will she possessed to keep from finding more mistletoe and dragging this man under it. She didn't want to be interested, but she couldn't seem to help herself.

How was she ever going to be able to hold her ground against Sam Hale?

She had *It's a Wonderful Life* playing on the TV, and the lights on the tree were the only illumination in the room. Anna took a sip of her cold, white wine and told herself to relax already.

Unfortunately, it wasn't working. Her mind kept turning to Sam Hale and what he might be up to. Since leaving his house that afternoon, she'd been trying to figure him and his plan out. So far, she had nothing.

When the doorbell rang, she groaned, pried herself off the couch and went to answer it. One glance through the peephole had her briefly resting her forehead against the door. Then she surrendered to the inevitable and opened it. "Hi, Clarissa."

Her father's wife scurried inside, fingers clutching at her shoulder bag. She glanced around the room, frowned, then reached over to flip the light switch. Anna blinked at the sudden blast of light.

"Oh, Anna," Clarissa said, "I just wanted to tell you how sorry I am for behaving so foolishly at the party. I didn't mean to embarrass you or anything."

"It's okay. I understand."

"I know you do, dear." The older woman patted her hair as if searching for a strand out of place. She was doomed to disappointment. Clarissa's short, bright red hair was, as always, perfect. "I'm just so worried about your father."

Which was the only reason Anna was willing to overlook Clarissa's panicky attempts at matchmaking. "Dad will be fine. The company's had rough times before."

"Not like this." Clarissa reached out, snagged Anna's wineglass from her hand and downed what was left of it in one long gulp before handing it back. "Thank you. But now that I know you're actually interested in Samuel Hale, I'm resting easier."

Here it comes, she thought. "Clarissa, there's nothing going on between—"

"No, no, I don't want to invade your privacy," she said with a careful shake of her head. "I just wanted you to know that I understand completely. It was so wise of you to move from Garret to Sam. After all, it's *his* company. Garret's just the younger brother."

Anna felt a headache coming on and wished for more wine to drown it. "I'm not *after* either of them. Sam..."

"Oh, we all saw the kiss," Clarissa assured her, letting

her gaze sweep around the small living room of Anna's bungalow cottage. She stared at the brightly lit tree for a moment and smiled before adding, "Your father is pleased, too. Though he does want to talk with Sam."

"No," Anna said quickly, imagining her father asking Sam's "intentions." "No talking. Clarissa you have to tell Dad that I'm not dating Sam."

"Why ever would I do that?" Clarissa smiled conspiratorially. "He only wants to know that you're happy, dear."

"Clarissa..."

"Oops," she said, with a quick check of her watch. "I really have to run. I'm meeting your father for an early dinner before we go to the community theater. They're doing *A Christmas Carol.*"

"Clarissa," Anna tried again, but her stepmother was already halfway out the door. "It's not what you think. Honestly, there's nothing between Sam and I."

She laughed. "Darling, I *saw* that kiss. Along with half the town, I might add. Whether you want to admit it or not, there's definitely something between you!" She leaned in, brushed a kiss on Anna's cheek and said, "Your tree's lovely, by the way!"

Then she was gone and Anna was left alone with her disturbing thoughts and an empty wineglass.

Five

She wasn't going to be painting in that wonderful room she had seen the day before.

Anna drove around to the back of Sam's house, following the long, wide driveway around the house to a sprawling lawn and what looked like a five-car garage. Trees lined one side of the property and the lawn sloped down toward the cliff and the ocean below. A white rail fence meandered along the cliff's edge and boasted a few late blooming chrysanthemums at its base.

Storm clouds hovered on the horizon, looking as though they were gathering strength to make a rush toward shore. A cold wind rattled through the boughs of the pines and snatched a few orange leaves from a huge maple tree. Winter in coastal northern California didn't mean snow after all. It meant fall-colored trees long into January.

It really was lovely, but why she was back here, she

didn't have a clue. The housekeeper had directed her to the back of the house and now, she wasn't sure what to do next. Anna got out of her car and looked around, pushing the wind-twisted tangle of her hair out of her eyes.

She walked back to the trunk of her small SUV and lifted the hatch, displaying all of her tools. Yardsticks, paints, transfer papers, charcoal sticks and painter's tape. Her brushes were standing straight up in empty coffee cans and she used a plastic caddy to hold a selection of pencils along with painters' rags and tightly closed jars of clean water.

Movement at the corner of her eye caught her attention and Anna turned to look. She hated the fact that her heartbeat jumped in her chest at first sight of Sam Hale striding from the garage toward her. Faded blue jeans hugged his legs, and he wore a dark green sweater and black boots.

She hadn't expected to have to deal with Sam while working here. Didn't he have things to do? Cars to build? Universes to run?

"What are you doing here?"

"I live here, remember?"

"Yes," she said on an irritated sigh, "I meant…"

"I know what you meant." He glanced into the trunk of her car. "You need *all* of this to paint a picture?"

"It's a faux finish, not just a picture," she told him, then added, "and yes, I do."

One corner of his mouth lifted and Anna hated to admit even to herself what kind of impact even that tiny half smile of his had on her.

"Okay, then," he said, reaching into the trunk to pick up most of her equipment. "Follow me."

She didn't have much choice, Anna thought, trotting

behind him in an attempt to keep up with his long-legged stride. He led her toward the garage and headed directly for an open doorway. She followed him inside and glanced down the long open space at the cars parked in separate bays. There were two of them and they were really just shells. No tires, no engine, no window glass.

"You couldn't afford one with an engine?"

He grinned at her and the solid slam of that smile hit her hard enough to momentarily dissolve her balance.

"Those are great cars," he pointed out after he set her supplies down onto a neatly organized workbench.

"If you say so."

"I thought artists had great imaginations," he taunted.

"I use it for painting, not for driving."

"When I get that Bentley and the Cobra up and running, you'll change your tune."

Confused, she looked again at the skeletal cars. She hadn't known that he was a man to actually get his hands dirty. All she'd ever heard of Sam Hale was that he designed luxury cars that his company built for the bored rich. "You work on them yourself?"

"I do. Got my start that way," he said with a sigh of satisfaction. "I was a mechanic," he told her, shaking his head in memory. "A damn good one. Worked night and day when my folks died to make sure Garret could go to college and have a good shot at life."

"What about your shot?" she asked, surprising herself as much as him.

He shrugged. "I did the college thing, but it was cars that drew me in. I built my reputation slowly, growing my business and then I built a custom car for a Hollywood producer. He liked what I did so much that he recommended me to his friends. And before I knew it, I was running Hale Custom Autos. But I still like to work on cars myself, get my hands on a flatlined engine and make it purr again. Guess you don't understand that, huh?"

"Actually, I do," she mused and found herself looking at him in a whole new light. She'd assumed he was simply another wealthy man, locked in his office, running his own little world from the top of a pedestal. It seemed there was more to Sam Hale than she had thought. "Trompe l'oeil painters can use computer programs to design and detail out every move. But I'd rather get my own hands on a blank wall and make it something amazing."

"So," he said with that half smile she found so dangerously compelling, "you're telling me we have something in common after all?"

She looked at him, standing there all tall and dark and gorgeous. Seriously, he had enough charisma and magnetic attraction about him for two healthy men. She knew that for her own well-being, what she should do was say screw the job and the money and get back into her car. But she wasn't going to do that and she knew it.

"Yes," she admitted. "I guess I am."

For a brief moment, their eyes locked and the air between them practically sizzled. There was something here, she thought as her heart pounded and her mouth went dry. Something that was as exciting as it was dangerous. And she had zero business feeling this way about him. There was no way anything was going to happen between them.

He didn't trust her. He thought she was after his money. Well, to be honest, she was. At least what he was going to pay her for this job. And as far as Anna was concerned, Sam Hale was an overbearing, arrogant boob—except he apparently had unexpected depths.

With those thoughts ringing loudly in her head, she took a breath and shifted the subject to safer ground. "So, what exactly did you have in mind for your mural?"

"Business it is, then," he said, still studying her. "For now."

He walked to the small office area, separated from the garage by a half wall. There was a desk, two chairs, a single filing cabinet and a half-dead fern in a blue pot inside. The walls were white and blank. There was a skylight overhead, providing plenty of natural light, but there were no windows, which struck Anna as odd.

"I don't have a lot of windows in here," he said as if he knew exactly what she was thinking. "When I'm working on the cars, I like to keep the area as clean as possible. Don't want dust and dirt blowing in, but it gets claustrophobic in here after awhile."

"I can see why," she said, already studying the pristine white wall, letting her imagination kick in. "Can't you put in windows that don't open?"

He shook his head. "Dust can still get in with a loose seal or whatever. The skylights are double-sealed. Until I get down to serious work I can open the garage bay doors for air. But once the detail work starts, I'll be keeping the place shut up tight."

"Okay, do you want anything in particular?"

Another slow smile curved his mouth. "I can think of a couple of things."

"I'll bet," she said, taking a step back from him just for good measure. "But I was talking about the mural."

He shook his head. "I'll leave that to you. I just want to be able to look at something that makes me feel less closed in. Can you do it?"

"I can." She walked to her supplies and pulled out pencils, a yardstick and blue painter's tape.

"Do you need anything from me?"

"Just for you to go away," she said, knowing she'd never be able to concentrate if he was in the room watching her.

"You got it." He started out of the office. "I'll be working in the garage. If you need anything, let me know."

"You're working *here?*"

He smiled again and Anna felt that rush of something hot and wicked sweep through her one more time. She hadn't counted on having him underfoot all day. She'd expected him to leave her alone. The claustrophobic feel of the massive garage instantly notched up a level or two.

"I can run my company from here with a laptop and a phone," he was saying. "So until you're finished, I'll be right here. Every minute."

"Great."

He grinned and she knew he was enjoying her discomfort. Deliberately, she turned her back on him and went to work. If she could keep busy enough, she told herself firmly, she'd forget he was near.

Sadly, even Anna didn't believe that.

She sang when she worked.

Sam groaned and banged his head on the uplifted hood when he straightened abruptly. Rubbing the aching spot on his skull, he shot a glare toward the woman taking up far too many of his thoughts. He'd thought having her here would be a good idea. He could watch her. Find out who she really was.

Sam had thought about calling his brother to let him

know that Anna actually *did* have a price. But he decided against it. He knew Garret was over her, but Sam didn't want hard feelings between him and his brother. If Garret brought up her name again, Sam was simply going to point out to his younger brother that Anna had said flat-out that even though she hated him personally, she was going to take his money.

Wouldn't that prove once and for all that the gorgeous Anna was as mercenary as she was beautiful?

Wouldn't that prove to his brother that Sam had been right all along?

Only problem?

Sam wanted her.

Bad.

When his cell phone rang, he lunged for it, eager for a distraction. "Hale."

"You sound like you want to hit somebody."

Sam scowled at his brother's cheerful tone. It was Garret's fault that Sam was, at the moment, tied into knots. "You volunteering?"

"Hell, no," Garret said, laughing. "Just wanted to tell you I'm leaving town for a while."

"What?" Irritated, Sam wondered when the hell his younger brother was going to grow up. "You can't leave town. You've got a job."

"Oh, that didn't work out," Garret dismissed it easily.

"Damn it, Garret—"

"I didn't call for a lecture," his brother interrupted. "I'm heading to Aspen for a few days. Just wanted you to know, is all."

"Great," he muttered. "Thanks."

Garret sighed, clearly as irritated as Sam felt. "I don't want to fight with you, Sam. I just need some time, okay?

That job you got me at the advertising firm was making me nuts."

Sam thought about the favor he'd called in with a friend in San Jose and realized he'd have to make another call to his old friend. To apologize for his brother. "Garret, you said you wanted that job."

"It just wasn't me."

"What *is?*" Sam asked, unable to understand his younger brother's inability to find something he had a passion for. So far, all the younger Hale had been really good at was women and snowboarding. "What're you going to do for a living, Garret?"

His brother laughed shortly. "Don't worry," he said. "I'll think of something."

That was what worried him, Sam told himself silently.

"Look, I'll be back for Christmas. Promise."

"All right," Sam said, lifting his gaze toward the office where Anna's singing had quieted. "I'll see you when you get back."

Anna stepped out of the office. When he hung up, she asked, "Problem?"

"No," he said flatly. He wasn't going to discuss his brother with the very woman he'd forced Garret to stop dating. "How's it coming?"

She watched him for a second or two, then said, "Great. Want a look?"

He walked to the office, brushed past her and stared at the wall where blue painter's tape was applied in a series of arches and straight lines. Sam couldn't see where she was going with this, but she seemed happy enough with it. "That's good?"

"It is," she said, coming up beside him. "I'm almost

ready to start laying down some background color along with the outside detail lines."

"What is it?" he asked, watching her face rather than trying to make sense of the taped wall.

She looked up at him. "A surprise."

She was too close and smelled too good. Her dark red hair pulled back in a ponytail at the base of her neck, her bright green eyes glittered with excitement. Her blue denim jeans and oversize blue work shirt over a paint-stained black T-shirt somehow looked…perfect.

Sam had never seen a more beautiful woman. He was in deep trouble here and he knew it.

He just didn't care.

Before he could think better of it, he reached out, took her arm and dragged her close.

"Sam…" Her voice was a whisper.

"Don't talk, Anna," he told her and slowly bent his head to hers. He had to see if everything he'd felt when he first kissed her was still there.

She lifted one hand to his chest and he could have sworn he felt the heat of her palm slide down inside him, easing away the chill. "This isn't a good idea," she told him.

"You're still talking," he said.

"Right," she agreed, lifting her face to his. "Shutting up now."

Then he took her mouth with his, felt the hard punch of desire and knew that Anna Cameron was going to be way more trouble than he'd first believed.

Six

The next few days settled into a routine. Anna worked in the office, Sam worked on his cars and they met in the middle for lunch provided by his housekeeper. By silent agreement, neither of them referred to the blisteringly hot kiss they'd shared in his office.

But the memory was there. Haunting them. Keeping each of them so tightly wound that just being close to each other sent up sparks.

Anna didn't know what to do. She hadn't wanted or expected to like Sam, but he was getting to her. Slipping beneath her radar, worming his way into her thoughts. Heaven knew he had already breached her body's defenses. Anytime he came near, her heartbeat sped up and every square inch of her jolted into electric life.

But it wasn't just the desire, the passion; it was more. Over the last few days, they'd talked and even laughed. He'd told her about some of his more "eccentric" customers and she'd shared a few of the truly hideous murals some of her clients had asked for. She actually liked working in the office, listening to the sound of power tools as he refurbished one of his cars.

At the bottom of it, though, she had to keep in mind that he didn't trust her. He thought she'd been willing to seduce his brother to save her father's company and what did that say about him? But he'd also given her free rein to paint whatever she wanted in his office. That was trust of a sort, wasn't it?

Yet, she remembered all the things Garret had told her the night he broke things off with her. Along with the whole out-to-get-my-money speech, Sam had also told Garret that he considered artists to be flaky and emotionally unstable. So what was she supposed to make of that?

"None of this makes sense," she told herself, glad that the day was almost over. Sam had gone up to the main house half an hour ago and she'd heard Mrs. Soren leave shortly after. As soon as Anna finished this one section of the mural, she'd be leaving, too. Christmas was getting closer and she still had shopping to do. Besides, one of her own traditions was to wander through Crystal Bay at night to enjoy all of the Christmas decorations. She hadn't had a chance to do that yet and she figured tonight was as good a time as any.

She reached up and with her fingertips, quickly brushed the line of paint she'd just laid down, softening the edge and blending the paint into the other background colors so that it became a pale wash of blue and gray that would, eventually, be the sky in her mural. Stepping back, she nodded to herself, and wiped her fingers on the rag stuffed into her pocket. Then she stretched her aching shoulder muscles and swiveled her neck, trying to ease the tension there as well.

Satisfied she'd done all she could, she quickly cleaned her brushes and closed up her paints. The sudden roar of a powerful engine splintered the quiet and Anna stepped outside to follow the sound.

A cold wind slapped at her as she spotted Sam, astride a huge, gleaming black motorcycle. He grinned at her approach and revved the engine again, making the bike sound like a hungry lion.

He wore a battered, brown leather jacket and balanced two helmets and another leather jacket across his lap. He looked way too good, Anna thought, feeling that rush of heat swamp her again. There might as well have been a *Danger* sign flashing over his head. But she still couldn't seem to stop herself from walking toward him, like a moth headed directly for the tantalizing flame.

She shouted over the rumble of the engine, "What's going on?"

"We need a break," he said, his voice deep and loud enough to carry. "Put this on."

He held out the leather jacket and Anna knew she should say no and head back inside. Sunset was already staining the sky and she should be headed home. Back, she thought, to her empty apartment, a hot shower and a cold glass of wine. Then she looked into his blue eyes and knew that she wasn't going anywhere but with him.

She slipped the jacket on and zipped it up. Then she accepted the helmet he offered her and tugged it on as well. He grinned at her and her stomach did a slow bump and roll. He pulled on his helmet, flipped the visor down and indicated that she do the same. Then he shouted, "Hop on!"

Knowing it was most definitely a mistake, Anna did

just that. She climbed aboard the motorcycle, her thighs spread wide, aligning along his. She leaned into him and he turned his head to say, "Wrap your arms around me and hold on, Anna."

"Where are we going?"

"It's a surprise," he called back.

He'd already surprised her, she thought, feeling the rumble of the engine rippling throughout her body. She'd never been on a motorcycle before and she had a feeling that this trip, wherever he was taking her, was going to be memorable. She wrapped her arms tightly around his middle and inhaled sharply as he roared down the length of the driveway and out onto the road.

Sam drove along the coast road for miles, and Anna watched as night claimed the sky. Trees lined one side of the wildly twisted road and the ocean, dazzled by moonlight, lay on the other.

She'd never experienced such a thrilling sense of freedom before. Fear rode just below the surface of her excitement, but she refused to acknowledge it. Instead, she focused solely on the incredible sense of being as one with Sam and the machine carrying them both through the darkness.

He doubled back after a long while and she realized they were headed back to Crystal Bay. Disappointment rose up in her as she realized she wasn't ready for the ride to end. For the magic to be finished. Lifting one hand from the handlebars, Sam pointed into the distance and she shifted her gaze to follow the motion. Her breath caught as she saw the town of Crystal Bay, sitting on a crescent-shaped harbor, spreading back through the trees. In the surrounding darkness, the town's Christmas lights shone from a distance like jewels strewn across the ground. She smiled and felt a stirring of something magical rise up around her.

Soon, they were roaring down Main Street and Anna wondered if everyone they passed was speculating. Sam's motorcycle was well known and she was guessing that her long, red hair hanging out from beneath her helmet would be enough for most people to identify her. The question was, did she care?

No. At the moment, no, she didn't care. She loved the feel of being on the powerful Harley with Sam. It was a moment snatched out of time. They couldn't speak, so they couldn't argue. They were wrapped so tightly together, each of them could feel the heat of the other's body.

Her own heartbeat was hammering in her chest and she thought she felt a matching rhythm coming from Sam's body. Anna swallowed hard and rested her head against his broad back. Her grip on him tightened as the rumbling of the engine vibrated her body and jolted every already-sensitive nerve ending.

Christmas lights blurred into a stream of color as they whizzed past. Shoppers hurried along crowded sidewalks. Pine garlands were strung across the street from lamppost to lamppost. Carols pumped from one of the stores they passed and she smiled behind her helmet. The giant Christmas tree in the town square glittered, while overhead, stars slipped in and out from behind clouds.

She didn't know why he'd taken her on this ride, but she was so glad he had. Anna felt *alive* in a way she had never known before. She wanted this night to never end, but of course, it did.

He slowed the motorcycle down as they pulled into the driveway of his home. Light spilled from the windows onto the lawn in golden patches and Mrs. Soren's car was gone from its usual parking space.

They were alone and instantly, Anna felt tense. It had been so liberating, riding behind Sam, tearing along the coast. But now they were back and nothing had really changed between them. There was that amazing sense of chemistry that burst into life whenever they were together. But at the heart of things, they were on opposite sides of a figurative wall.

He hit a button on the handlebars and as one of the garage doors opened, he steered the bike inside. An overhead light came on with the opening of the door and when he shut off the engine, the silence was deafening.

Reluctantly, she released her death grip around his waist, ignoring the empty feel of her arms. She reached up to pull off her helmet and shook her hair back. Her voice was soft and nearly breathless as she said, "That was amazing, Sam. Thanks."

"You're welcome." He climbed off the bike, then took both helmets and set them on a nearby bench.

She was still sitting on the black leather seat, afraid to stand up for fear her legs wouldn't support her. The engine was off, but her body was still vibrating. In fact, it felt as though every cell she possessed was electrified. Her gaze locked with his and she took a long, slow breath.

In the pale light, his blue eyes looked gray and stormy. She was willing to bet that the same wild passions were shining in her own eyes.

"Sam—"

"Anna—"

They spoke together and then closed their mouths in sync. Anna was edgy and she knew it. There were too many thoughts running through her mind. Too many emotions clamoring to be noticed and acknowledged. Carefully, she swung her leg over the back of the bike and stepped down onto the gleaming garage floor.

She swallowed hard. "You know, maybe I should just go now."

"Don't."

Her gaze snapped to his. Every breath was a challenge. Her heartbeat was so frantic that she could hear the roaring pound of it in her own ears. A damp, hot ache settled between her thighs at the same time tension gathered in her chest. She wanted to whimper with the force of the want nearly choking her. But acting on what she—*they*—were feeling wouldn't solve anything. Wouldn't change anything. It would only make things worse.

"Sam, you know as well as I do that I should leave."

He shook his head. "I don't want you to and I don't think you do either."

"It's not about want." *Unfortunately,* she added silently.

"It's all about want," he answered, walking toward her with slow, deliberate steps.

Every step that brought him closer to her sounded like a gunshot in the quiet. Anna's pulse was racing and her breath was now chugging in and out of her lungs. When he was close enough to touch her, Anna instinctively leaned in toward him. Her better judgment was being tossed aside. While a still-rational corner of her mind warned her that she was making a mistake, a much more powerful voice within told her to take what he offered. She knew then she wouldn't be leaving. Not until the desperate ache inside had been eased.

He scooped both hands into her hair, cupping her head

in his hands, then he drew her closer, lowered his head and kissed her. Anna was done for.

Plain and simple, Sam Hale swept all common sense right out of her mind. He silenced that warning shriek inside her and awakened the part of her that wanted. Needed.

She was blistered by the heat racing through her. She welcomed it, moved into him and wrapped her arms around him. Nestling as close to him as she could, Anna gave him everything she had.

Their tongues tangled in a fierce dance of desire. Breathing became secondary to the rising tide of passion erupting between them. Hands moved, explored, claimed. Bodies melded and whispered words of hunger rattled through the silence.

Finally, he tore his mouth from hers, stared down into her eyes and demanded, "Come with me."

She met his gaze, saw exactly what she needed to see and knew that denying him wasn't an option. Because she didn't want to leave. She wanted to feel as alive as she had on the back of that motorcycle—alone in the dark with *him*.

"Yes," she said softly. "Now."

Hand in hand, they raced across the yard, Sam's longer strides forcing Anna to run at his side. She laughed shortly, the sound escaping into the night and dissolving like soap bubbles.

He opened the back door, drew her inside and closed the door behind them. Swinging her up against him, he held her so tightly she could hardly breathe. Yet she didn't care. All she cared about was his mouth on hers, his hands stroking up and down her back in a proprietary manner that absolutely thrilled her.

"You taste so damn good," he murmured, breaking away to nibble at the base of her throat.

She sighed because she didn't need words to tell him what she was thinking, feeling. He just knew.

He slid his hands up under her shirt, skimming his fingertips across her skin until she was shivering in his arms. Then he smiled down at her and said, "Not in the kitchen, damn it. Upstairs. In my bed."

Here was her last chance, that tiny voice in the back of her mind whispered. Last chance to back out before she made what could be an incredible mistake. She stared up into those amazingly blue eyes of his and nodded. "Yes, Sam."

He grinned, swept her up into his arms and headed for the hallway.

"I can walk," she said on a laugh.

"Your legs are too short," he countered. "I'm faster."

"Good point." She snuggled into him, kissing his neck, the underside of his jaw. Her hands slid across his chest and she felt the pounding of his heart beneath her palms.

He took the stairs at a dead run and rushed her down a dimly lit hall so quickly that she noticed nothing. Then he was stalking into his bedroom and Anna took a quick look around.

Boldly masculine, the furniture was big, dark and heavy. Deep blue drapes were pulled back, allowing the moonlight to pour through the wide windows to lay across a bed big enough for four people to sleep comfortably.

But sleeping wasn't on her mind.

He set her on her feet and instantly reached to pull off his shirt. Anna watched and took a short, sharp breath at the first sight of his broad, bare chest. Muscular and tanned, he actually rippled when he moved and she wanted nothing more than to be held against that expanse of warm, golden skin.

In seconds, they were naked. Sam tugged the navy blue duvet off the mattress and then they were tumbling onto the cool, crisp sheets. He seemed to be touching her everywhere at once. Her body was humming with sensation and her mind fogged over as he dipped one hand to her core and cupped her heat.

"Sam..." She lifted her hips into his touch, seeking more, needing more.

He leaned on one elbow, looking down at her, watching her eyes as she twisted and writhed beneath his touch. She read a desperate craving in his eyes and that only served to inflame her own desires.

He dipped one finger into her warmth and she groaned, lifting into his touch. Her hands moved up and down his arms, nails scraping along his skin. His thumb caressed that one small nub of sensation until Anna felt as though she were about to splinter into a million jagged pieces.

Her breath was strangled as she fought to reach the pinnacle that was waiting for her. She needed it. Needed him. "Sam, please. Now. Inside me."

He dipped his head and took one of her nipples into his mouth, licking and nibbling, before suckling at her until she felt the draw of his mouth all the way to her toes. She grabbed at his shoulders, then stabbed her fingers through his thick, dark hair. Holding his head, she drew his gaze to hers and whispered, "I need you, Sam."

"I've got to have you, Anna. All of you." He shifted then, moving over to kneel between her parted thighs. Scooping his hands beneath her bottom, he lifted her off the mattress and as she fumbled for something to hold on to, he covered her aching heat with his mouth.

Anna hissed in a breath and closed her eyes only to open them again an instant later. She wanted to watch him. Wanted to see as well as feel what he was doing to her. His lips and tongue moved over her flesh with a deliberation that pushed her higher and higher. He tasted her, licked her and took her to the very peak of that release she knew was waiting for her.

Then he pulled back and left her dangling over the precipice.

"Sam!" She called his name in a broken voice and heard the desperate need in her tone. "Don't you dare stop now," she warned.

That smile of his curved his mouth as he shook his head. "Not stopping, Anna, just shifting gears."

He laid her down on the mattress, caught her gaze with his and entered her body in one long, smooth stroke. She gasped, arching into him. He filled her completely and as her body stretched to accommodate him, she lifted her hips into him to take him deeper.

"Easy…" He whispered it, the word almost strangled. "You start moving and this is going to be over way too fast."

She smiled up at him, and pulled his face to hers for a kiss. "I'll take my chances."

"My kind of woman." He kissed her back as his body moved into hers, setting a fast rhythm that she eagerly matched.

He pushed her higher and higher and Anna felt herself spinning completely out of control. She'd never known anything like this. This was so much more than she'd expected. So much more than anything she'd ever experienced.

It was magic, she thought wildly. The very magic she'd dreamed of finding one day. And it was more than the incredible chemistry they shared, Anna thought with a start. She was falling for Sam Hale—and there was no way that this would end in anything but misery.

Sam had already told his brother that she wasn't, in effect, "good enough" for him. So why would she be good enough for Sam himself?

Heart suddenly aching, she looked up into his eyes and was held, spellbound as she shattered. Her body clenched around his and she held him tightly to her as he followed her into the sensation-filled abyss.

Seven

"You slept with him."

Anna hadn't expected the truth to be quite so obvious, but she shouldn't have been surprised. Tula had gotten home from visiting her cousin and had come straight over to talk, bringing a bottle of wine with her. Now that they had the wine poured and were settling in for a good talk, Tula had taken about five seconds to blurt out her suspicions.

Anna blinked at her friend but didn't bother to deny the obvious. "How could you tell?"

"You're practically radioactive you're glowing so brightly," Tula said as she plopped down on Anna's living room couch. "Man, go away for a few days and the whole world tips on its axis. I thought you hated Sam."

"I thought so, too," Anna muttered and dropped onto the other end of the sofa. Shoving both hands through her hair, she shook her head. "Honestly, I don't know how this happened. He made me so mad at first and then, we started talking and he's really funny and nicer than I thought and he kisses so well and before you know it, we were on his motorcycle looking at Christmas lights and then we were at his house and in his bed and *boom*."

Tula stared at her for a long moment before whispering, "Wow."

"Yeah, wow." Anna shifted her gaze to the Christmas tree, where a few packages lay in a bright carpet of color. Shaking her head, she idly said, "I don't know what I'm going to do."

"You're in love with him, aren't you?"

"I don't know—" She said it automatically, then stopped herself. "That's a lie. Yeah, I am. For all the good it'll do me."

"Oh, Anna, it could work out."

She smiled, in spite of the growing sense of dread inside. "I don't think so. He didn't think I was good enough for his brother, remember?"

Tula waved that off with a sniff. "Please, you were way too good for Garret."

Anna laughed. She'd always been able to count on her best friend. Still, she couldn't shake the feeling she'd had since leaving Sam's bed the night before. That she was on borrowed time and that she was feeling a lot more for him than he was for her. There was simply no way this was going to end well.

"Thanks for that," she said, reaching out to squeeze Tula's hand. "But I'm tired of thinking about me. Tell me why your cousin Sherry wanted to see you so badly."

Tula sighed and reached to the coffee table for her glass of white wine. "You're not going to believe this, but Sherry's pregnant."

"Really? Who's the father?"

"I don't know," Tula said and took a sip of her wine. "She refused to tell me. But what's worse, she hasn't even told the guy he's going to be a father."

Anna couldn't imagine keeping something like that to herself. "Why would she do that?"

"I don't know." Tula frowned. "I told her that if the guy was worth sleeping with, he's worth telling him the truth, but she wouldn't listen."

"So why'd she want to see you?"

Tula leaned back into the couch. "She wanted to name me the legal guardian of the baby just in case something happens to her."

"But she hasn't even had it yet."

"You know Sherry. Afraid of everything. Although," Tula said, "she's not scared of raising a baby alone, which would absolutely terrify me."

"Did you agree to be the baby's guardian?"

"Sure I did," she said. "We're family."

"So," Anna told her, picking up her own wine, "we've each had a busy few days, huh?"

"Guess so," Tula agreed. "Though yours, I'm thinking, was way more fun."

The next few days were a blur of stolen moments and passion hot enough to burn a man to a cinder. Sam dreamed of Anna at night and thought of nothing but her during the day. Every time he was with her, he wanted her more.

Scrubbing one hand across the back of his neck, he kicked the wall behind his desk and hardly felt the pain. He'd come into the office to avoid Anna at home. He couldn't see her without wanting his hands on her and he couldn't think when he was touching her.

How the hell could Sam lay claim to Anna when he

had practically forced his brother to walk away from her? Would his brother ever forgive him? Could he risk losing his only family on the chance that what he and Anna had was lasting?

"Mr. Hale?"

He looked up as his assistant opened the door. "What is it, Kathy?"

"A Mr. Cameron here to see you."

Shock had him speechless for a second or two, but he recovered quickly. "Send him in."

Sam stood up to greet Anna's father and the older man shook his hand with a wary look. Suddenly, Sam felt a little uneasy. After all, he was sleeping with the man's daughter. "Good to see you, Dave."

"Sam." The man glanced around the spacious office before settling his gaze on Sam's again. "I won't take up much of your time. Just thought we should have a little talk."

"About what?" Oh, he *knew* what.

"Anna."

"Ah."

"Crystal Bay's a small town," Dave was saying. "Secrets are impossible to keep. So I figure we both know what's going on."

"Meaning?" Sam asked, unwilling to give any information on the off chance that Dave was still in the dark.

The older man frowned at him. "*Meaning,* I know you've been seeing my daughter just as you know my company's in trouble."

"Dave…" What the hell was he supposed to say? He knew Dave Cameron was a proud man.

He lifted one hand in a bid for silence. "Whatever's between you and Anna is your business. You're both adults. What I'm here to tell you is, contrary to what everyone in town is thinking, I won't use my daughter as a bargaining chip for business."

Scowling himself now, Sam took a deep breath. "And I wouldn't use her either."

Dave studied him for a long minute. "Then we understand each other?"

"I think so," Sam said, bristling a little under the man's close scrutiny.

"Fine, then. I'll wish you a good day and be on my way." Dave started for the door, then stopped and looked back. "One more thing. You hurt my little girl and we'll be having another talk."

The man was gone before Sam could respond. But then, what could he possibly have said? He felt like a damn teenager after a dressing-down. The hell of it was, he had the feeling he'd deserved it.

Christmas was just a few days away when Anna finally finished the mural in Sam's home office. She could admit to herself that when she'd begun this job, she'd actually considered giving him some ghastly painting. A horrific view out an artificial window. But that idea hadn't lasted more than a moment or two. Her own professionalism prevented her doing anything less than her absolute best.

And now that she stood back to get the full effect of her work, she had to admit that she'd really outdone herself this time.

She was glad of it, too. Now every time Sam looked at this wall, he would think of her. It was the perfect goodbye. Because she'd come to the conclusion only the night before that what was between them had to end.

There was no future in it. And she was only hurting herself. Falling for Sam Hale had been inevitable. But she wouldn't stay with him, knowing what she did about how he really felt about her.

Sex between them was incredible. She knew he felt the same way. But desire was a long way from any kind of *real* feeling. She'd been deluding herself into thinking that something could come of this, when the truth was, he would never allow himself to care for her because when it came right down to it, he didn't trust her.

Well, she couldn't keep fooling herself. It was better to get out now, while the pain was still livable. If she waited any longer, she knew the loss of him would kill her.

Pasting a bright smile on her face, she closed up the last of her paint jars, tucked them away in the carrier, then took a breath. Steadied as much as she was going to be, she opened the office door and called out, "Sam? I'm finished. You can see it now."

He looked up from the car he was bent over and smiled at her. Anna's heart jolted and she knew she would miss that smile of his.

"The big secret revealed, huh?" He wiped his hands on a towel, tossed it across the car fender and headed her way. "Can't wait."

She stepped back so he could enter and shifted her gaze to his face as he saw the finished painting for the first time. His eyes widened and his jaw dropped. He couldn't have had a more perfect reaction.

"That's incredible," he said, walking closer to it.

"The ocean's still wet, so don't touch," she warned.

"The ocean's always wet, babe."

"Very funny."

Still shaking his head, he leaned in closer to the wall. "That's really amazing, Anna." He shot her a look over his shoulder. "I'm impressed."

"Thanks."

It had turned out well, she thought, studying her own work objectively. A gracefully arched window, shadowed from an unseen sun, opened up to a seascape that looked as vivid as life. Blue-gray sky, storm clouds on the horizon. Waves crashing against rocks, sending spray so high that it dotted the painted-on glass of the open window. A tumble of flowers and vines spread across the window sill, dripping color and motion onto a still life that made it seem all the more alive and real.

"What's this?"

"Hmm?" She glanced to where he was pointing. With a shrug and a smile, she admitted, "I was a little angry with you when I painted that part."

"Yeah, I can see that."

He grinned anyway, though, so Anna was glad she'd left in the snake with Sam Hale's features peeping out from the vines on the windowsill.

"You," he said as he walked toward her with a familiar glint in his eyes, "are a very talented woman."

"Thank you," she answered, her voice hardly more than a whisper.

He pulled her into his arms, dipped his head to kiss her and then seemed to notice her hesitation. "What is it?"

She should tell him now, Anna thought. Tell him that whatever was between them was over. But damn it, she wanted one more time in his arms. One more glimpse of the magic before she turned her back on it forever.

"Nothing," she said and reached up to wrap her arms around his neck. "It's nothing."

Then he kissed her and she forgot everything but what he made her feel.

Her body blissfully humming with remnants of plea-sure, Anna turned her head on the pillow and looked at the man beside her. How had she come to feel so much for him in such a short amount of time? And did that really matter? The simple truth was, she loved him and every moment she spent with him was only setting herself up for disaster and pain.

She had to end this while she still could.

"Sam," she said abruptly into the quiet, "this isn't going to work out."

He grinned, rolled to his side and slid one hand down the length of her naked body, making her shiver even as new fires erupted inside.

"Seems to be working just fine."

"No," she insisted, rolling out from under his touch. If she didn't say something now, she never would. Scrambling off the bed, she stood up and reached for her clothes. "It's really not."

"What are you talking about?"

She had his attention now, she thought, looking down into beautiful blue eyes that were narrowed in suspicion.

"Just that we can't do this anymore," she blurted.

"Why the hell not?"

She tugged her shirt over her head and shook back her hair. "I can't keep being with you when I know exactly what you really think of me."

He pushed off the bed and stood naked, facing her. He was amazing-looking and Anna had to fight hard not to be distracted. "What? What do you mean what I think of you?"

This was harder than she had expected it to be, but Anna kept going. She told herself that pain now would save her misery later, so it was best to just get this done so they could both move on with their lives.

"I *mean*," she told him, "Garret told me exactly what you said about me. Not only do you think I'm after him for money, but that you consider me flaky and immature and—why are you *laughing?*"

He shook his head, grabbed up his jeans and tugged them on. "Because this is so stupid."

"Oh, thanks very much."

"I didn't say *you* were stupid," he muttered, then spoke up more loudly. "Why is arguing with women so frustrating? The flaky and immature thing? That's not what I think of you. It's what I think of Garret. He refuses to grow up and I'm starting to wonder if he's even capable of it."

Only slightly mollified, Anna said, "But you did think I was after your money."

He didn't deny it. What would be the point? They both knew the truth. After a second or two, he said, "Okay, yeah. I did. Why the hell else would a woman like you be dating Garret?"

"You really believe I could do something like that? Use someone? Barter myself?"

He scowled and folded his arms over the chest she'd been draped across only moments ago. "I don't have to remind you that your father's company is failing—or that I've got more than enough money to save it."

"No," she assured him haughtily, "you really don't."

"Stop being so damn insulted. You wouldn't have been the first woman to use sex to get what you wanted."

She fisted her hands at her hips. "And is that what I'm doing now? With you?"

He glared at her. "How the hell am I supposed to know? You tell me."

Stung to the heart of her, Anna's unshed tears nearly blinded her. She stepped into her shoes and lifted her chin to match him glare for glare. "If you really do think so little of me, then I was wrong about you from the beginning."

He didn't say a word, just stood there, watching her. With every pulse beat, another tiny piece of Anna's heart broke away and shattered. Gathering up what dignity she had left, she said quietly, "I never want to see you again. You can mail me a check for my work."

"Fine," he answered quietly.

Before she left, she took one last jab. "When you're in your office, I hope you look at the snake often and remember why it has your features."

Eight

Christmas Day was just awful.

The Cameron family holiday breakfast was strained as Anna watched her father strive to remain cheerful despite the deepening worry lines at the corners of his eyes. Clarissa made a big show of a supposed "cold" that kept her constantly sniffing and wiping her eyes with her handkerchief.

And Anna missed Sam desperately.

She hadn't spoken to him in days, which only told her that she'd made the right decision. Sam had no doubt realized that they were better off apart. Truth didn't make the pain any easier to live with, though.

Yet, watching her father go through the motions on a holiday he loved was unsettling. She was worried enough about him that her own pain was taking a backseat.

After an exchange of presents, Anna joined her father in his study for a cup of coffee. Clarissa excused herself to take some cold medication.

"Dad," Anna said, sitting beside him on the brown leather sofa, "is it really so bad?"

Her father frowned and Anna knew she was crossing into unexplored territory. Ordinarily, her dad preferred that she and Clarissa be happy and completely ignorant of his business dealings. But after a moment or two, he gave a resigned sigh.

Patting her hand, he admitted, "It's not looking good right now, honey."

"Is there anything I can do?"

"I don't want you worried about this, understand?" He gave her tight smile. "Things will work out as they're supposed to. I'm sure the new year will bring plenty of opportunities."

Her heart already aching from the loss of Sam, Anna felt another wrench. Her father had worked hard his entire life to build a company he was proud of. Was he really going to lose it? And if he did, what would it do to him?

"No sad faces," he chided, leaning in to kiss her forehead. "We've got some Christmas cakes to eat, remember?"

Another family tradition. Decadent cupcakes covered in Christmassy icing were always eaten after breakfast in the Cameron house. She watched her father fight past his own disappointments and worries and knew she could do no less.

"Yes, we do, Dad. Want me to go get them from the kitchen?"

"Please. Take them into the living room by the tree." He stood up, still smiling tightly. "I'll just give Clarissa a hand finding her cold medication and we'll join you."

"Okay." There was a knot in her throat but she wouldn't let her father down. If he wanted to have a normal Christmas morning, then that's exactly what they would do. As he started walking away, though, she said, "I love you, Dad."

His smile was warm and real as he answered, "I love you, too, Anna. Now don't worry, all right?"

She nodded, though her concerns were still there. But she wouldn't contribute to her father's worries, so she silently vowed to keep her anxiety well-hidden.

"Have you heard from him?" Tula asked later that night over a Christmas dinner of takeout tacos.

Because Tula had no family, the two of them always had Christmas dinner together—with only one rule. Nobody cooked. So every year, they looked around for any restaurant that happened to be open. This year, it was Garcia's Familia. The food was terrific, but Anna wasn't enjoying it anyway.

Hard to eat when it felt as though there was a ball of lead in the pit of your stomach.

"Sam?" Anna shook her head and took a sip of wine. She pushed the tines of her fork through the Mexican rice as if drawing a picture. "No. And it's better that way. Really."

"Yeah," Tula told her. "I can see that. This is working out great for you."

Sighing, Anna set her plate on the coffee table and sat back on her couch. Her gaze fixed blankly on the brightly lit Christmas tree, she wondered what Sam was doing. If he missed her as much as she missed him. And she wondered how he had become so important to her in such a short length of time.

"Anna, you're miserable. Why don't you call him?"

She glanced at her friend and ruefully shook her head. "What would be the point? Nothing's changed. Even if it's not a conscious notion, he still thinks I'm after him for his money."

"That's crazy," Tula said with a snort of derision. Picking up her wine, she took a drink and said, "You had a fight. People always say things they don't mean in a fight."

"Or the truth comes out," Anna suggested. She'd already had this same conversation with herself a dozen times. She'd thought about that last fight from every angle and each time she came to one conclusion. "Either way, it's just over."

The phone rang, but she didn't move to pick it up. She didn't feel like talking to anyone anyway. Her heart hurt, not just for what she'd lost in Sam, but for her father. And there was nothing she could do about either situation.

"You're not going to get that?" Tula asked.

She shook her head. "Let the machine pick it up."

Which it did a moment later. She listened to her outgoing message and then her heart jolted at the sound of Sam's voice.

"Anna?" His deep voice sounded commanding. "If you're there, pick up."

Tula waved at her frantically, but Anna shook her head again. She had to curl her fingers into fists to keep from reaching for the stupid phone, but she did it. She couldn't talk to him. Not now. Maybe not ever again. It was hard, but it would be even more difficult if she didn't stay strong.

Sam sighed into the phone, then said, "Listen, I, uh, wanted to say merry Christmas—"

Anna's heart tugged a little at that and the twisting pain made her close her eyes. If things had been different, Sam might have been here right now, with her and Tula, having dinner and laughing. But things weren't different and they weren't going to be.

"Talk to me, Anna. Don't let it end like this."

"Oh, God," she whispered.

When she still didn't pick up, he muttered something unintelligible and hung up.

"Yeah," Tula said, every word coated in sarcasm, "I can see why you don't want to talk to *him*. Sounds like a heartless bastard."

"You're not helping," Anna told her.

"This time," her friend said sagely, "I think you're going to have to help yourself."

Sam glared at the damn phone as if Anna not speaking to him were its fault instead of his own.

"*Idiot*," he muttered thickly, shoving one hand through his hair. He'd done nothing but think about Anna for the last few days. Their last argument was on constant replay in his thoughts. And every time he relived it, he saw the shock on her face and the hurt in her eyes. He still wasn't sure how the damn argument had erupted and he'd like nothing better than to step back in time and bite back the words that had hurt her so badly.

Why the hell had he said something so stupid? He knew damn well that she wasn't after his money. He had been convinced of that as soon as he saw how much time and effort and artistry she'd poured into the mural she had painted for him. No mercenary woman would have cared so much about doing a good job. She would have come in, slapped some color on a wall and cashed his check.

But Anna had pride. Integrity.

And *his* heart, damn it.

He poured a Scotch and took a seat on the sofa. The

Christmas tree was lit up and soft jazz pumped through the stereo. It would have been perfect, he thought. If Anna were there.

Instead, there was a hollow spot in his chest that he couldn't see being filled anytime soon. God, if he had to live the rest of his life with this emptiness inside...

"Sitting alone in the dark?" Garret said when he came into the room. "Not a good sign, Sam."

"It's not dark," he protested lamely. "The tree lights are on."

"Yeah." Garret grabbed a beer from the wet bar, then sat down in a chair close to his brother. He took a long drink and said, "So, you want to tell me what's eating you?"

"What?" Sam shot his brother a look.

"I was gone like a week or so, not years. You're..." he tipped his head to one side and studied Sam "...different, somehow. Still mean as hell, of course, but there's something else, too."

This was a rare moment, Sam thought. His younger brother was noticing something outside himself. And maybe it was a sign that the younger Hale brother was finally taking a step toward maturity. God, he hoped so. Because Sam knew what he had to do.

He'd missed Anna like he would have an arm or a leg. Somehow, in the last couple of weeks, she had become as necessary to him as breathing. And he couldn't live without her. So he had to tell his brother that not only wasn't Garret going to get Anna back, but also that Sam was in love with her himself.

Love.

Wasn't the first time he'd thought that word over the last few days. But it was the first time he'd welcomed it. And admitting the truth, if only to himself, made him feel…good. He looked at his brother and knew that what he was about to say could cost him the relationship. But he had no choice. He had to try to make things right with Anna.

"Actually," Sam said, setting his glass of Scotch aside. He sat up, and braced his forearms on his thighs. Looking directly into his brother's eyes he said, "There is something else."

Garret paled at the suddenly serious tone. "Are you okay? You're not sick are you?"

"No." Sam laughed shortly and realized it was the first time he'd even smiled since losing Anna. That thought steeled him for what came next. "Nothing like that. But you remember when I told you to break up with Anna Cameron?"

Garret rolled his eyes. "You mean when you ordered me to stop seeing the man-hunting gold digger? Yeah, Sam. I remember."

Sam bristled, hearing his own words tossed at him. God, he'd been an idiot. "She's not, you know. A gold digger."

One of Garret's eyebrows lifted and he took a swig of his beer. "Interesting. I seem to recall trying to convince you of that."

"Yeah, well. Things have changed."

"I'm getting that. So let's hear it." He sat back, kicked his legs out in front of him and crossed his feet.

Sam couldn't sit still. He jumped up and paced to the wide front window where the Christmas tree lights were reflected on the glass. Staring out at the night, he started talking.

"I was going to get her back for you," he admitted.

"What?" Garret jolted upright. "Just a minute—"

"*Was,*" Sam repeated, turning now to look at his

brother. "Look, I didn't mean for this to happen, to go around you like this, but the truth is, I'm in love with Anna."

He waited, letting his words sink in. Watching his brother's face, Sam didn't miss the wide smile or the relieved sigh.

"Thank God."

"Excuse me?" Sam said.

"I don't want Anna back, Sam." Garret blew out a breath.

Now Sam was confused. He'd thought his brother had real feelings for Anna. "But I thought—"

"Is this what's been bugging you since I got home?" Garret asked, standing up to walk to his brother's side.

"Well, yeah." Sam hadn't expected their little chat to go so well and damned if he could figure out why it was. But he was grateful, as well as surprised.

"Then relax, brother," Garret said and clapped him on the shoulder. "I'm *entirely* over Anna. I mean, I knew she wasn't after the family money, but she wasn't for me anyway. That's the only reason I went along with you telling me what to do. I mean, come on, what am I? Twelve?"

Sam scowled at him, but realized he should have considered that before. Garret never had done anything he didn't want to.

"I'm glad for you, Sam. You're a way better fit with her than I ever could have been. She's nice and everything, but she's too traditional for me."

"Traditional." Sam laughed, still stunned by his brother's reaction. "And you told her I thought she was flaky and immature."

Garret laughed, too, then shrugged. "Well, I wasn't going to tell her that you had called *me* that."

Sam looked at his younger brother and felt a rush of love for him. Didn't matter if Garret hadn't found his way yet, Sam was suddenly sure that he would. Now all that was left was for Sam himself to find a way back to Anna.

"Is it just me?" Garret wondered aloud. "I thought love was supposed to make you feel good and you still look crappy. What's going on?"

He scrubbed one hand across the back of his neck and stared out at the night again. "Anna's not real happy with me right now."

"Ah, that explains it."

Sam shot a look at his brother. "What?"

Garret grinned. "Why the snake Anna painted on your wall has *your* face."

"Yeah, that's a long story."

"Why don't you tell me about it?" Garret said. "We'll have another drink. And then I'll tell you all about the professional snowboarder I met in Aspen."

Sam shook his head and smiled. "What's her name?"

Garret winked. "Shania. She's gorgeous. And amazing—brilliant, talented. She's really something special. And in two days, we're flying to Geneva for a couple of weeks to do some serious boarding."

Sam pulled his brother in for a brief, hard hug, then let him go again. "I'm not gonna worry about you anymore, Garret," he said with a smile. "I think you're going to do just fine."

Garret's features sobered and he nodded as if accepting an award. "Thanks for that, Sam," he said. "I really will be all right, you know. So now that I'm off your worry list, why don't you tell me all about Anna and we can figure out a way to get her back in your life?"

"I'll tell you," Sam said, draping one arm over his

brother's shoulders to steer him over to the chairs. "Then you can tell me all about Shania. As for me, I'm doing whatever I have to to get Anna back."

Nine

Christmas was over and New Year's Eve was just a day away. Anna had buried herself in work, wishing away the holidays, wanting to get lost in the dark, gray days of January. A storm was settling in over Crystal Bay and the cold damp suited Anna's mood perfectly.

Maybe her father was right. Maybe the new year would be filled with lots of opportunities. But at the very least, time would be passing. And the more time passed, the easier it would become to get over Sam.

At least, that's what Anna fervently hoped.

"For now, though," she told herself firmly, "I'm going to concentrate on work and try to put everything else out of my mind."

Sounded good in theory, but Sam's image would never completely leave her thoughts. He was with her, sleeping and waking. He was always there, just behind the mental door she tried repeatedly to close.

"How's it coming, Anna?"

"What?" She jolted and her grip on the paintbrush in her hand tightened. Whipping around, she looked at Mateo Corzino as he walked toward her. The owner of Corzino's, home of the best lasagna on the California coast, Mateo had hired her to do a mural on the wall of his restaurant.

It was a big job that could keep her busy for a couple of weeks. He wanted a view of a Sicilian harbor, fishing boats tied up at a dock, complete with cliffs and sand-colored buildings in the background. And he wanted it to look as though the view was seen through a crumbling wall. She was eager to dig in, loving the challenge and a crumbling wall was one of her favorite effects. If only she could fully concentrate instead of having her heart and mind torn in two.

"Jeez," he said with a grin, "didn't mean to scare you."

"Sorry." She shook her head and laughed a little. "I guess I was just thinking so hard I didn't hear you come up."

He glanced at the wall where she'd just begun laying down the dark brown tracer lines that would eventually look like cracks in old plaster.

"It already looks real," he said, a touch of awe in his voice. "I don't know how you do it."

Pleased, Anna smiled and wiped her fingers on a paint rag. "Well, I don't know how you make that amazing sauce of yours either, so we're even."

"Speaking of that, I'd better get back to the kitchen. My wife's minding the stove *and* the baby." He looked at the wall again and nodded in appreciation. "You need anything, you give a shout. The restaurant won't be open until dinner, so no one will bother you."

"Thanks, Mateo," she said, but he was already gone, hurrying back to his family. She heard a deep baby giggle coming from the kitchen and then Mateo's wife laughed along.

Anna sighed and turned back to her paints. Emptiness filled her as she reached up to paint another jagged line on the wall. As she did, she felt as though she were capturing in paint the cracks in her own broken heart.

She worked for another hour or two uninterrupted. Then she heard a frantic knocking on the glass door behind her. Anna ignored it, figuring that Mateo would be rushing out to take care of an overeager customer. But when the knocking continued, Anna sighed, and stepped out from behind a tall, potted ficus tree.

Clarissa was standing outside the restaurant, leaning up against the glass, shading her eyes so that she could look inside. A second later, that frantic knocking started up again.

Mateo finally headed out of the kitchen and Anna stopped him. "I'll take care of it, Mateo. Sorry."

"Oh, sure," he said, recognizing Anna's stepmother. "No problem."

Anna hurried to the door, turned the lock and opened it. "Clarissa, what is it? What's happened?" Then she saw her stepmother's eyes were red and swollen, tears streaming down her face. Grabbing hold of the woman, Anna demanded, "Is it Dad? Is he okay?"

Clarissa nodded, gulped audibly and lunged for her. Hugging Anna tightly, she tried to talk around her own tears, but the words were garbled.

Relieved that her father was all right, Anna patted the woman's back until she calmed down, then pulled away and said, "What's going on, Clarissa? Why are you crying?"

"Oh," the woman said, rummaging in her black bag for a handkerchief, "it's just so wonderful…"

Anna's heart picked up a normal rhythm. Not bad news, then. She waited impatiently for her stepmother to wipe her eyes and blow her nose. Then, at last, Clarissa spoke again.

"I had to find you, Anna," she said. "Tell you right away. I know how worried you've been for your father and you just had to know the good news."

Patience, Anna reminded herself, though the opposite feeling was pumping through her fast and hard. You needed patience with Clarissa.

"If it's good news," Anna said softly, steering Clarissa to a chair, "then I definitely want to hear it."

But Clarissa didn't want to sit down. She stopped suddenly, gave Anna another hard, tight hug and stepped back, giving her a brilliant smile. "Thank you, Anna. I don't know how you did it, but thank you."

"I don't understand," she said, feeling that hard-won patience begin to dissolve. "What are you thanking me for?"

Clarissa's eyes widened and her smile got even brighter.

"You don't know? I can't believe you don't know," she said. "I thought for sure you were behind this somehow, but now…"

Anna took a breath and blew it out again. "Honestly, Clarissa, I do love you, but if you don't tell me what's going on soon—"

"Of course, of course." Clarissa grabbed hold of Anna's paint-stained hands and said, "It's Sam Hale. He contacted your father yesterday…Hale Luxury Autos has signed an exclusive contract with Cameron Leather." Her tears started again in earnest, but her brilliant smile never wavered. "Your father's company is safe, Anna. He's so relieved. So happy. I thought you had talked to Sam about this. Somehow arranged it all and I had to come and thank you for whatever you'd done."

"Sam called Dad?" she echoed, her heart jumping into an accelerated beat. She hadn't talked to Sam in days, but he'd called her father. Done this to help her father.

Hope leaped to life in her chest and she silently prayed that this meant what she thought it might. Dazzled, confused, Anna realized that Clarissa was talking again and forced herself to pay attention.

"He did. They met this morning with Sam's and your father's lawyers and settled it all in an hour. Everything's taken care of and, oh, Anna, it's so wonderful to see your father really happy again." Clarissa reached out and hugged Anna tightly before letting her go. "It's as if a boulder had been rolled off his shoulders."

"Why would Sam do this?" Anna wondered aloud, not really expecting an answer. Was it possible that he did feel more for her than want?

"I don't know, dear," Clarissa said softly. "I thought he'd done it for you."

Why would he, though? she asked herself. Why, when she'd broken it off with him, refused to take his calls? Why would he do something so wonderful?

Anna tore off the oversize apron she normally wore when she was working. Bunching it together, she passed it off to Clarissa and said, "I have to go. Will you tell Mateo I'll be back?"

"Going to Sam?" Clarissa asked softly.

"Yes," she said, frantic now to see him. She had to know why he'd done this. Had to know if he felt even half as much for her as she did for him.

"Good for you, honey," her stepmother told her, reaching out to pat her cheek. "You go on. I'll tell Mateo. But come to the house for dinner tonight, all right? I know your father will want to share this with you. We can celebrate."

"I will, Clarissa," Anna said and impulsively kissed the woman's cheek.

Hopefully, she thought as she ran out the door, there would be a *lot* to celebrate.

Ten

Sam cursed as he jammed his thumb on the undercarriage of the Bentley. Should have known better than to be out here working, he told himself as his thumb throbbed in time to his heartbeat. His mind wasn't on the work and that was a recipe for danger.

But as he'd given his staff two weeks off, he hadn't been able to face going into an empty building. Instead, he turned and went into the small office off the garage. He stood in the doorway, staring at the painting Anna had completed what now seemed like a lifetime ago.

The illusion of the ocean view was so clear, so real, he half expected to feel a breeze sliding through that painted-on window. Then his gaze dropped to the hidden snake peeking out of the flower vine. He scowled as he realized that he'd deserved to have her immortalize him like that. Damn it, he cared for her and he hadn't told her. He'd let his own suspicions drive her away when all he really wanted was her. Here. Now.

"This isn't helping," he muttered, trying to find something to do. Something to occupy his mind so it wouldn't automatically turn to—

"I thought I'd find you here."

He went still as a post. Her voice came from behind him and he'd hungered to hear it for so many days, he wanted to just take a second to enjoy it. But when she didn't speak again, he turned around to face her.

Her long, auburn hair was pulled into a ponytail and she was wearing paint-stained jeans and a black sweatshirt, also decorated with splotches of paint. Her eyes were locked on his and Sam thought he'd never seen anything more beautiful.

Behind her, he could see that the promised rain had finally arrived. The sky was gray and trees were bending in the wet wind.

"I went to your office first," she said.

He just looked at her. He couldn't seem to get his fill. "I closed it until after the holidays."

"Yeah, I saw the sign." She walked closer, the heels of her boots tapping in tandem with the rain.

It took everything Sam had not to go to her, wrap his arms around her and hold on. He wanted her with an ache that had only gotten more overpowering over the last few days. And he knew unless he had her in his life, he was doomed to misery.

"You've got paint on your cheek," he said.

She shrugged. "I'm working at Corzino's."

He nodded and wondered why they were suddenly being so damn polite.

"I know what you did," she said and walked close enough that he could smell her. The scent of her shampoo mingled with the sharp scent of paint and he almost smiled. Because to him, that was the essence of Anna.

"And?" he asked, staring down into her emerald green eyes.

"And, I want to know why," she told him softly.

"You know why," he admitted, his blood stirring, his body quickening. She was so close and he'd missed her so much.

After his meeting with Dave Cameron, he'd known that he'd have to face Anna. But he hadn't been sure what her reaction would be. Hell, she was a hard woman to predict, which was only one of the reasons he was crazy about her.

She watched him through guarded eyes. "I hope I do. Why don't you tell me?"

Grumbling now, he admitted, "I did it because I love you, okay? You wouldn't answer the damn phone and I knew you wouldn't see me. So this was the only way I had to tell you."

"Sam…"

"It's not the only reason," he told her, talking fast now that he had her here and it was so important to make her see what he was feeling. "Your dad's a good man and it's a good business decision for both of us, but you're the main reason I did it, Anna. I did it because of you. *For* you."

When she didn't say anything, he added, "I don't expect anything from you. You don't have to do anything. Hell, I don't even expect you to believe that I love you, but I do."

She still wasn't talking, and Sam suddenly couldn't stand still under her gaze. He grabbed her, giving into the instinctive urge clawing at him. He pulled her close, stared down into those green eyes of hers and said, "I'd do anything for you, Anna."

He loved her.

Anna sighed, grinned up at him and threw her arms around his neck, holding on for all she was worth. "Oh, Sam, I love you, too. I love you so much."

"God." He buried his face in the curve of her neck and swept his big hands up and down her spine, as if reassuring him that she was once again in his arms.

He kissed her, long and deep, and Anna felt her world right itself again. Fires burned inside her and she knew that with him in her life, she would never again be cold.

"You could have said something," he accused, when he finally broke the kiss long enough to look down at her. "Did you have to let me keep babbling?"

She grinned and leaned into him, arching her body into his. "Sorry. But after you said you loved me, I sort of zoned out."

"Is that right?" His voice was low and almost seemed to rumble along her nerve endings.

"Yeah, it is. I do love you, Sam," she said, staring into his eyes and letting him see everything she was feeling. "And what you did for my dad—you didn't have to."

"I know that," he said, and bent to kiss her again. Once. Twice. "I wanted to do it, not because I had to but because I knew it would make you happy."

"You make me happy, Sam. Just you."

"I'm making that my mission in life," he told her. "Because I never want to be without you again, Anna."

"Never," she whispered and sighed as he kissed her again and again.

At last, though, he pulled back and pointed at the mural. "This is the first time I've come in here since you left," he admitted. "I couldn't look at that painting without thinking of you. Couldn't look at that snake without remembering that I'd let you go."

She laid her head on his broad chest and smiled at the steady beat of his heart. "I'll paint over that snake," she promised.

"No," he told her. "Leave it. It's a good reminder to me."

"Of what?"

"Everytime I see it, I'll remember how close I came to losing you, and that'll make me appreciate what we've got together even more."

Tears filled her eyes as she smiled at him. "Tell me what we've got, Sam."

"Everything, Anna," he said. "Marry me and we'll have everything."

"Yes." She didn't have to think about it. Didn't have to wonder. Didn't have to ask herself if she was sure. It didn't matter if she'd met him two weeks ago or two years ago. This was the one man for her. The man she would love for the rest of her life. "Yes, I'll marry you."

One corner of his mouth tipped into that delicious half smile she loved so much. "Just what I wanted to hear."

His hands swept under the hem of her sweatshirt to cup her breasts and she groaned at the contact. He tweaked her nipples through the lace of her bra and Anna sighed in pleasure.

"I know a great way to spend a rainy day," he said.

She sighed, and almost surrendered before she remembered, "Oh, I can't! I have to work. I told Mateo and—"

Sam kissed her again until she couldn't think, let alone speak. When he lifted his head, he smiled down at her. "It's okay," he said. "We've got tonight to celebrate."

She winced and groaned aloud as she remembered she'd already made a promise to her stepmother. "I promised Clarissa I'd go to the house for dinner. To celebrate. You have to come, too, so we can tell them our news together."

He laughed and rested his forehead against hers. "Dinner with the family. Agreed. And I should probably have a talk with your dad about us anyway. But *after,* it's just you and me."

"Absolutely." She couldn't wait to get him alone. To feel his body sliding into hers. To hear him say he loved her again and to know that she would be with him forever.

"Since we missed our first Christmas together," Sam was saying, "we've got some catching up to do."

"What did you have in mind?" she asked a little breathlessly.

"Well," Sam said, "I'm thinking we'll have some wine, sit in front of the Christmas tree and open our presents."

"Presents?" she asked, confused.

He dropped his fingers to the snap of her jeans and flicked it open. Anna gasped as he undid her zipper and slid one hand across her abdomen. Then she understood.

"Ah. *Open* our presents," she said, moving into his touch. "Yep, that's a great idea. We could even call it our first tradition."

"You really are my kind of woman," he mused, zipping up her jeans and snapping them closed again.

"And don't you forget it," Anna told him, her insides melting at the wild, wicked look in his eyes.

"Not a chance, babe." Taking her hand in his, he kissed her knuckles, then said, "Come on, I'll drive you to Mateo's. I don't want you taking chances in this rain."

Anna hugged him and whispered, "Rain? What rain? All I can see is sunshine and rainbows."

While the rain pelted down from a steel-gray sky, inside the garage there was warmth and love and the promise of tomorrow.

Sam held on to her for another long minute, giving each of them a chance to settle. To relish the realization that they were together now and everything was going to be just as it should be.

"Happy New Year, Anna."

"Happy New Year, Sam."

* * * * *

MISTLETOE MAGIC

SANDRA HYATT

To the wonderful women and men of RWNZ
and especially Barbara and Peter Clendon.

One

The babble of chatter and laughter ceased.

The only sounds left in the sudden hush of the living room were the rich baritone of Bing Crosby crooning "I'll Be Home for Christmas," and the crackle of the fire in the stone fireplace.

Perplexed, Meg Elliot turned, careful not to spill the pyramid of Christmas tarts from the silver tray in her hands.

And came face-to-face with a stranger.

Face-to-chest, actually. She had to look up from the navy polo shirt stretched across his shoulders to see his face. Dark, wavy hair, in need of a cut, brushed his forehead. He was clean-shaven and tanned. Too tanned for this time of year at Lake Tahoe, and not a skier's tan. But it was the silver eyes boring into her with unreadable intent that stilled her.

She knew those eyes.

But she didn't know this man.

She'd met so many people in the last few months, it was no surprise that she might forget a face. Except for the fact that this man was not the forgettable type—imposing, disconcerting and way too handsome.

How had he even gotten in? Caesar, guard dog extraordinaire, invariably created an unholy ruckus when anyone, even her friends, approached the house. It had taken him all of the three months she'd lived here to get used to her. And the stranger standing in front of her, silent and watchful, most definitely did not fall into the category of friend. He dropped a leather overnight bag to the carpet with a quiet thud.

There was something so expectant in the way he and, she realized, her guests, watched her. And waited.

The seconds ticked by. Who was he? She needed the answer to that single, simple question before she knew how to react.

He glanced up. Above her hung a chandelier, and incongruous among the glinting crystal dangled a sprig of mistletoe.

Surely not?

Meg looked back at him, looked again into those eyes.

Eyes she'd only ever seen the likes of once before.

She felt the color drain from her face. He eased the tray from her hands, placed it on the table behind her. "Luke?" His name left her lips on a whisper.

He watched her struggle for calm, and his mouth stretched into a smile that held little humor. He slid large hands over her jaw to cup her face. "Hi, honey, I'm home," he said softly as he lowered his head.

Too stunned to react, Meg stood rooted to the spot.

Warm lips collided with hers. There was hunger in his kiss, hunger and a quest for control.

She wouldn't react. Wouldn't *let* herself react.

His fingers threaded into her hair as he claimed her mouth in a blatant attempt to dominate her, and then he gentled his kiss. That surprising gentling melted her defenses and dissolved rational thought.

He was alive. He was home. He was kissing her again.

He'd kissed her only once before. She'd thought her memories had been colored by the circumstances of the time.

Apparently not.

This kiss was every bit as beguiling and as latent with promise as that first one.

But the moment she found herself kissing him back, reaching for him, he lifted his head and then set her away from him as though it was she who had initiated the kiss and he needed to put distance between them to prevent her from doing it again.

Dimly, she heard a burst of applause.

Her awareness returned. Her guests—the organizing committee for tomorrow night's charity dinner—were witnessing this scene play out. She felt the color rush back to her cheeks.

Luke's gaze didn't leave her face. "Aren't you going to introduce me, darling? I saw only a few familiar faces."

Not daring to look away, she said, "Everyone," and the word came out a hoarse whisper that made him grin a shark's grin. She cleared her throat. "This is Luke Maitland. My husband."

Then it all happened in a blur: hugs, congratulations, assurances that they knew she'd want to be alone with her husband after his unexpected return. Within minutes she and the stranger she'd married stood together at his front door as the quiet purr of the last departing vehicle faded into the night.

Meg stepped out and away from the arm he had draped possessively and firmly—as though he knew she wanted to bolt after that final car—over her shoulder. Frigid air wrapped itself around her in its stead.

He followed close as she led the way back to the high-ceilinged living room. His living room. Platters of nibbles still sat on the coffee table, Bing still sang, but everything had changed.

Those eyes. How could she not have known him instantly?

Finally, when the silence had stretched way beyond comfortable, Meg spoke. "You're looking...better." The last time she'd seen him he'd been lying, pale and unshaven, on a makeshift hospital bed on an Indonesian island. And taller. In the few days she'd spent with him, he'd invariably been lying down, or bent with pain when he'd tried to stand. Illness had a way of diminishing people. There was nothing diminished about him now. Upright and strong, he comfortably cleared six foot.

"Disappointed?" he asked quietly.

The question stunned her. "No! How can you ask that? I thought you might die."

"So did I. But that wouldn't necessarily have worked out badly for you." He glanced around the sumptuous living room.

They'd spent only a few days together, but she'd thought she'd had a bond with the observant, insightful man in her care. A man who, despite his pain, had made her laugh. The man she remembered had been nothing like this—cool and distant. Suspicious. Then again, the man she remembered had been close to death. "No, it would have worked out terribly."

His gaze never wavered. "You got my house. It could have been permanent. And you'll have realized by now that there's much more than the house."

Back then, he'd talked only of the beauty and magic of the area, of how he'd wanted someone who could appreciate it to have it, someone who understood him. She'd had no idea when she'd married him just how wealthy he was, that when he'd said house he meant mansion on the shore of Lake Tahoe, complete with private jetty, indoor pool, game room, boardroom and a library stocked floor to ceiling with books. She could have lived happily for years in the library alone.

Meg crossed to the fireplace and positioned herself behind an armchair, her fingers pressing into the padding of its high leather back. "You have no right to just walk in here—"

"To my own house?"

"To just walk in," she continued, "and start accusing me of...what exactly is it you're accusing me of?"

He paused and she held her breath, waiting, uncertain. "Nothing," he said on a rough sigh, dragging a hand across the back of his neck, and some of the accusation leached from his eyes.

"Luke, it was all your idea. You practically demanded I marry you."

He strolled closer, picked up one of the Christmas cards from the mantelpiece and glanced at the inside before replacing it. "I don't remember much more than a token resistance from you."

"You were sick, so let me help you remember. As I recall it, you were desperate. You even invoked the memory of your mother."

She'd met his mother only once. Meg had gone with a friend to hear her speak at a lunchtime fundraiser in L.A. and had been so impressed that she'd introduced herself to her afterward. They'd ended up having coffee together and talking for hours. It was as a result of that one fateful meeting that when things had ended between Meg and her then-boyfriend she'd thought of doing something completely different. Had thought of Indonesia and the Maitland Foundation. A path that had led her to here and now. "You asked me to do it for her—because of how much I'd respected her and because I knew how revered she'd been on the island. And you even threatened that if I didn't accept you were going to propose to the very next woman who walked into the room." She'd believed him to be serious and in an uncharacteristic fit of possessiveness Meg hadn't wanted anyone else to have "her" patient, the man she'd spent so many hours talking to. "You said I was doing you a favor."

Hard to imagine how that could be true now, how plain Meg Elliot, with little to call her own, could have done a handsome millionaire a favor by marrying him.

He rested an arm on the mantel and stared at the fire. A smile touched his lips and then vanished. Uncomfortable in the same room as the stranger who was her husband, Meg edged around the chair and toward the door. She needed space, needed to get to her own room and process what was happening, figure out what she did next. His return changed everything.

"You must be tired." She had no idea where he'd come from or how far he'd traveled today. But it was late and deep lines creased the skin around his eyes, so she assumed her guess had some foundation. "We can talk all this through in the morning."

Luke straightened and strode to the door, cutting off

her exit. "You're right. I am tired." He looked down at her, then lifted his hand to twist a lock of her hair around his finger. "I take it our bed's in the master bedroom."

Meg swallowed. "Our?" He was joking. Testing her. She was sure of it. Almost one-hundred-percent sure. Ninety-eight at least. Even if she had been the type of woman someone like him would be attracted to, theirs had been an arrangement of practicality and desperation. An arrangement that they'd agreed would end when he returned home.

"You got the benefits of being my wife. Surely I get some benefit in being your husband?"

She pushed his hand away and squared off to him. "You got benefits. Because of me, your brother hasn't moved into this house already."

"Half brother," he corrected her. "And that wasn't the benefit I was thinking of."

"It was when you married me. Or maybe you didn't care about there being any benefit to you, but you most definitely cared about making sure Jason didn't benefit. Cared enough to marry a stranger."

"A stranger with the gentlest hands."

Meg stilled.

"I thought about those hands as I was recuperating."

His sudden change of tone and topic disconcerted her and she took a step back. He was still trying to dominate her, unsettle her, this time with words. That was all it was. She couldn't let him know the effectiveness of his strategy, how very unsettled she was. She, too, had thought about her hands on him.

"You have a lot to explain to me. Where have you been? Why haven't you been in touch before now?"

He watched her steadily. "Nagging me already?"

"Legitimate questions."

"I have several of my own."

"Understandably. So I suggest we both get a good night's sleep and deal with them in the morning. The guest wing is that way." She pointed down the hallway.

"The guest wing? In my own house?"

"My things are in your room. I'll shift them out tomorrow. But for tonight, yes, you can have the guest room." Over the lonely months Meg had imagined many possible scenarios for Luke's homecoming—they had varied from tender to joyful to passionate.

This tension-laden standoff certainly hadn't been one of them.

Luke watched his wife's pretty blue eyes as he searched for the familiar in her face, searched for the differences. Time was, women jumped at the chance of going to bed with him. Although admittedly he was a little out of practice. Still, appalled horror was definitely a first for him.

He'd dreamed of this woman. And granted, many of those dreams had been the product of delirium. Many, but not all. The others had been the product of good old-fashioned desire. He hadn't known whether that attraction was merely the product of time and circumstance.

And he still couldn't answer that question for sure. Different time, different circumstance and he could still feel the pull of the woman standing in front of him.

Who was this woman he'd married?

He recognized the irony in his situation. Most of his life he'd kept people at a distance and now he had a wife he scarcely knew.

He reached for the tendril of golden-brown hair that curled against her pale throat. She blocked his hand, wrapping slender fingers around his wrist. "Afraid of me, Meg?" Her scent was something floral. Innocent. And distracting.

She dropped his wrist, lifted her chin and her wide clear eyes searched his face. Defiance overlaid a glimmer of wariness. "Should I be?"

He could still feel the imprint of her fingers, her skin against his. It had been like that whenever she'd touched him. "What do you think?" He didn't know why he was goading her. He'd had scarcely more than a few hours' sleep in the last forty-eight hours. All he really wanted was to lie down somewhere, he didn't care where, and close his eyes. He'd come home, not knowing what to expect, but knowing she couldn't have been as simultaneously wholesome and desirable as his memory wanted to paint her. Besides, he'd never really been into wholesome.

"I think, no."

He hadn't even known if he'd be able to find her. He certainly hadn't expected her to be hosting a party in his own house. It tarnished the wholesome image, made him doubt his judgment and his memories. "You're sure?"

"I think, for some perverse reason, you'd like me to be afraid of you. But the man I remember was decent and kind."

He watched her lips, a soft coral pink. He hadn't intended on kissing her. But her lack of recognition of him had galled. And besides, she had been standing under the mistletoe. What was a husband supposed to do? "I was sick. I wasn't entirely myself."

"Some things don't change."

Another first, someone defending him to himself. "And some things change completely, Mrs. Maitland." For instance, he now had the wife he'd sworn he'd never burden his life with.

"I'm not Mrs. Maitland. I never took your name. It didn't seem right."

He didn't know whether he was relieved or affronted. "Just my house. My money. My life." He curled his hand around the newel at the base of the stairs.

Her eyes narrowed and her hands went to her hips. "You're swaying, and talking almost as much gibberish as you were that last day on the island. Go to bed."

"Come with me." He was in no state to do anything other than sleep. But she didn't know that. "I've been sleeping alone for so long."

"Luke." She said his name with such frustrated impatience, and none of her earlier trepidation, that maybe she did know.

"That wasn't how you used to say my name." He'd heard her the times when she'd thought he was sleeping. And even when she'd known him to be awake, there had been such tenderness in her voice. "And not how I dreamed of hearing you say it."

"First my hands, now my voice. Any other parts of me you dreamed of?"

Luke smiled. "I don't think you want to know." Color climbed her cheeks.

TWO

Luke woke alone in a broad, soft bed. Nothing unusual about the alone part, but the bed was a different story altogether. The snow-white sheets smelled fresh and clean and felt crisp against his skin. A feather pillow cushioned his head. Opening his eyes, he scanned the room. A miniature Christmas tree stood on the dresser. Christmas?

Then he remembered last night. Though he'd been so exhausted, it was all a little vague. Coming home. Finding Meg, the woman he'd married out of desperation and anger, here. And he remembered the mistletoe. *That* memory was crystal clear. He also recalled his last sight of her hurrying up the stairs away from him.

Throwing back the covers, he strode to the window and pushed the curtains wide, needing to orient himself to the time and the season. Outside, ponderosa pines framed a panoramic view of Lake Tahoe. A leaden sky hung low and oppressive with the threat of snow but gave no real clue as to the time of morning.

He stretched, easing his shoulder through a full range of movement. It was his shoulder that had started it all. A gash from a handsaw dropped from the roof of the almost-completed school building. In the heat and humidity the cut became infected. The infection steadily worsened. And the remote Indonesian island's depleted medical supplies hadn't run to the antibiotics he'd needed.

He'd only gone to the island to fulfill a long overdue promise to his mother to take a closer look at the Maitland Foundation's work there. She'd headed up that office until her death a year ago. But while seeing the foundation's work, he'd discovered his half brother's duplicity. And the visit had nearly ended up costing his life.

He'd also discovered Meg.

And got himself a wife.

A wife he now had to un-get.

A movement on the path leading up from the lake toward his house caught his eye. His wife. Meg. Not Meg Maitland. But Meg…he couldn't even remember her surname. Wearing sweats and a form-fitting, long-sleeved top, with her hair tied into a high, swinging ponytail, she jogged along the path toward him, her breath making small puffs of mist in the air. Caesar trotted at her side, a stick in his mouth. His dog at least had known him last night, even if he now seemed more than happy with his allegiance to her.

She glanced up, saw him, then averted her gaze. Was he—? Luke looked down. He wore boxers—one of his few purchases on the way home. So, what was her problem? Whatever it was, she definitely wasn't looking back his way. She tossed the stick for Caesar and when he returned with it, she bent over and fussed with him for a while before disappearing round the side of the house.

Fifteen minutes later, Luke, showered and fully dressed, rummaged through his kitchen cupboards looking for something to eat. The pantry was better stocked than he ever remembered it being.

At the sound of footsteps, he turned. She, too, had showered and now wore appealingly snug jeans and a red-and-white sweater. She looked fresh and innocent, like she ought to still believe in Santa Claus. But looks could be deceiving. He had a lot of questions for her. Questions he intended to get answers to today.

He hadn't exactly behaved with his trademark calm detachment last night. A fact he regretted. But he couldn't quite bring himself to regret kissing her. It might have been his only opportunity. Soon she would be out of his house and out of his life. That's what they'd agreed should happen if—when, she'd insisted—he came back. Though they hadn't discussed time frames.

"Do you want me to make you lunch?" she asked.

"Lunch? I usually start with breakfast."

A smile twitched at her lips. "After midday, I usually call it lunch."

He remembered that smile, how easily and often it played about her mouth, how it made her blue eyes sparkle like sunlight on water, reminding him of the lake he loved. Making her smile had been one of his few pleasures when he'd been laid low. "You're kidding me." He knew he'd been tired, but…he searched the kitchen. The clock on the microwave read one-forty. And he knew that wasn't a.m.

"You must have been exhausted." She watched him warily.

He nodded.

"Sit down. I'll make you a sandwich."

Was she was trying to soften him up, being all sweet and obliging, this woman installed in his house, his life? Did she want something from him? Of late, it seemed everyone—friends, enemies, officials—wanted something.

His cynicism must have shown because her hands went to her hips. "Oh, for goodness' sake, sit down." She pointed, straight-armed, at one of the bar stools behind the breakfast bar. "I'm not going to try and poison you and I don't want anything from you. I'm offering—and it's a one-time-only offer—to make you lunch. While you look infinitely better than you did back on the island and much better than you did last night even, to be honest, you still don't look great. And as from now, I'm going to refuse to care."

Luke smiled as he strolled to take the seat he'd been ordered to. So, his Florence Nightingale wasn't all sweetness and light. He liked her better for it. It made her more real. He watched her moving about his kitchen, opening and shutting cupboards and the fridge with what he deemed unnecessary force. She didn't bother asking him what he did or didn't want on his sandwich, which didn't bother him, because he was so ravenous he didn't care.

He'd never sat here and watched a woman in his own kitchen before. He wasn't sure he liked it.

Gradually, her movements slowed and gentled to something practiced and efficient as she set about putting the sandwich together for him. He watched her deft hands with their delicate fingers, watched the sway of her hips and the curve of her rear as she crossed the kitchen for this or that, and decided that a woman in his kitchen wasn't entirely a bad thing. A few minutes later, she slid the plate across the breakfast bar toward him.

"Thank you."

The simple courtesy seemed to surprise her, which shouldn't surprise him. He hadn't exactly been Mr. Charming last night. Or this morning.

Luke turned his attention to the sandwich. He was halfway through it when a cup of coffee materialized beside his plate. He looked up and met her gaze. Her earlier stony expression had softened. "Thank you," he said again.

And was rewarded with a soft smile and felt again a glimmer of the brief connection they'd once shared. "You're welcome. You still drink it black?"

He nodded. Not that there'd been the option of having it any other way of late. She turned her back on him and adjusted the radio till she found a station playing Christmas carols. She wore her hair out and the soft curls brushed just past her shoulders. He'd never seen it out before. On the island, for practicality's sake, it had always been tied up. And last night, apart from that single tendril she'd allowed to curl beside her throat, it had been twisted into something fancy at the back of her head. He hadn't realized that it was quite so long or silky and his fingers itched to touch it, to know the feel of it. He clenched his fists and his jaw. Hair was hair. He did *not* want to know how hers felt. What he wanted was to get his life back to normal.

And that did not include having a wife in it.

She'd made herself a coffee, too, and picked up her cup, cradling it with two hands as she leaned back against the counter on the far side of the kitchen.

Luke returned his attention to his sandwich and didn't

look at her again until he was finished. But when he did he found her gaze still steady on him.

"You were hungry?"

"Apparently."

"I can make you another one. Or get you some fruit."

"It's my house, Meg. I can look after myself."

She bit her bottom lip.

"So, tell me——" They both spoke at once.

"You first," she said.

"Tell me about the last three months."

She shrugged. "I left the island, came back here. It took a while to convince Mark of the truth of my story and that your letter to him hadn't been signed under duress. Putting in the tree house incident was what clinched it. He figured you wouldn't have told that story to anyone you didn't trust. Even at gunpoint." Her eyes danced.

"And you're now the only person in the world apart from Mark and me who knows."

"My lips are sealed." She pressed the lips in question together.

But they hadn't always been sealed like that. They'd parted for him last night. Let him into her warmth.

"Mark was great. He went along with everything, helping explain my presence to your friends. Apparently, you're so deeply private that no one was surprised they hadn't heard of me. Only pleased to meet me. And Mark helped me look for you."

How hard had they looked and how much had Mark—his attorney and his friend—helped her?

Kind, intelligent Mark. In those moments Luke had tried to be altruistic, he'd thought that if he didn't make it back, Meg and Mark might be good for each other. He wasn't feeling altruistic now. Far from it.

A too-familiar tension started to build. It was getting old, the second-guessing, the not knowing who to trust. "Do you want to walk?" He needed to get outside, to get moving.

And he needed to remember who his friends were. They weren't many but they were true. And Mark was one of them. Luke had no need or right to doubt him.

As for Meg, he wanted to trust her, but the jury was still out on that one. In reality, he'd known her only a few days in Indonesia and he'd been perilously ill most of that time. His judgment couldn't possibly have been sound. He'd been betrayed before by people he'd thought he knew. And he didn't truly know why she'd agreed to marry him.

"Sure." Gentle, trusting. She gathered up their few dishes, put them in the dishwasher, then followed him to the front door.

He opened the closet wondering whether his jacket would still be there. It was. On the same peg he always hung it on. The first one. So, she hadn't got rid of his stuff or even moved it for her own convenience. He'd wondered how much of his presence she'd expunged from the house when she'd kept him from his bedroom last night.

A red jacket hung beside his. He reached for it and the scarf hanging with it, passed them to her, then held open the front door.

As she walked past him, he caught the scent of her hair, green apples, and he had to fight an urge to stop her so that he could lower his head and inhale that freshness, inhale some of her seeming innocence. The sort of innocence a man could want to take advantage of.

"Jason hasn't bothered you?" Because Jason, his half

brother, was exactly the type of man who would take a perverse pleasure in abusing innocence.

She hesitated. "Depends on what you mean by bothered?"

He pulled the door shut behind them. "Care to explain?"

They walked down the stairs together. "He comes around a lot. At first he was suspicious, a little bit antagonistic even. He had a lot more questions than anyone else about our relationship and our…marriage. And he seems to come round only when no one else is here."

At the foot of the stairs, she bent to pat Caesar, who'd bounded up, joyous at the prospect of another outing. Luke was sure his dog—part Alsatian, part something that really, really liked to fetch sticks—used to have more dignity, but he'd dropped to the ground and rolled over for Meg to scratch his belly. She had nice hands, delicate and gentle. And soothing. And he would not think about her hands. Specifically, he would not think about her hands on him. She straightened. "I gather I'm not the type of woman you usually dated."

"I guess not. You're definitely shorter." Meg barely came up to his chin. Her eyes narrowed suspiciously but she didn't say anything and he fathomed the reason for her skepticism. The last woman he'd dated was Melinda, an ex-model, willowy and glamorous. Who wouldn't in a million years have even contemplated a six-month stint of voluntary work in third world conditions. That was, in essence, the biggest difference.

"I met your last girlfriend."

"You did?" He couldn't imagine the two of them having anything in common. He started for the path and she walked at his side.

"She called around one day and Jason arrived just a

few minutes after. He told her I was your wife, although I suspect she'd heard something to that effect already. And then he told me she was your ex-girlfriend."

And wouldn't Jason have enjoyed that spot of stirring. "How did she take it?"

"She smiled."

"That's good," he said hopefully. Melinda had broken it off with him several months before he'd gone to Indonesia. She had no cause to be upset.

"It wasn't a happy smile."

"Oh."

"I know it's none of my business, but why did you and her break up?"

Maybe she had a little cause. He cleared his throat. "Because I didn't want to get married."

"Which kind of explains the not-so-happy smile."

"I guess."

"She was very beautiful." She said it with a kind of awe. But as beautiful as Melinda had looked, she had nothing on Meg, whose source of beauty had nothing to do with the clothes she wore and everything to do with what shone from within.

"Perhaps you should explain to her why you married me," she said quietly.

"I'll think about it." He couldn't see that it would achieve anything, but Meg seemed to want it. Maybe to ease her own conscience. She seemed so earnest. So innocent. "How old are you?"

A grin tilted her lips and coaxed one from him in return. Admittedly, it was an odd question to ask his wife. "Twenty-eight," she said. Nearly ten years younger than him. A world of difference in age and cynicism. Maybe it was that openness to her that made her look so young, so appealing.

Meg broke their tenuous connection as she turned away and continued walking toward the lake. "I learned your age from our marriage certificate."

That piece of paper legally binding them. He'd need to set about *un*binding them as soon as possible, because despite their verbal agreement that she'd leave when he got back, she was legally his wife. She'd have rights if she chose to exercise them.

She'd helped him, he owed her something. Certainly more than mere gratitude. How much more would be the pivotal question. And Mark would no doubt have an opinion on that as well as the most efficient and effective way to undo what he'd done. Set them both free. "What day is it?"

"Saturday."

He'd call Mark on his personal line later, set up a meeting for first thing Monday morning. The sooner that was sorted, the better. Regardless of how much she was likely to cost him. In the meantime, he'd be friendly but distant. He didn't want to alienate her. But on the other hand, he didn't want to encourage her to think there was anything more to their marriage than her having the use of his house until his return. He also needed to talk to Mark about Jason.

At the water's edge, they negotiated age-old granite boulders. As she clambered between two rocks, he offered his hand. Her glance flicked to his face, she took his hand—hers cool and fragile in his—and then eased it free as soon as the need passed, sliding it into her jacket pocket. He could almost want it back. He shoved his own hands into his pockets. "You were telling me about Jason. That at first he was suspicious…" Jason was an unscrupulous slimeball with a talent for ferreting out people's weaknesses. But he hid that side of his nature well and knew how to ingratiate himself with people.

"Then something changed. Once he accepted our… marriage," she glanced away as she said the word, "…he got a whole lot nicer, started offering to help me with things. But he had a lot of questions about where you were, why you weren't home with me. I'd told him, like you suggested, that you'd stayed on to straighten out things with the charity on the island and that you'd be home in a couple of months."

The track along the shore narrowed, forcing them to walk close, down-padded shoulders occasionally brushing. "Did you accept his help?" he asked.

"What do you mean?"

"A simple question."

"But there was something weird in the way you asked it, like you were accusing me of something."

"I wasn't accusing you of anything. Jason's offers of help have been known to take many forms."

"I don't really understand why you hate him so much. He can be a bit creepy, but he's had a tough life."

Not like you. The implication was clear. That was how Jason had got to Luke, too, playing the sympathy card, explaining how hard done by he'd been because of Luke's dead father, *their* father, a man who'd never acknowledged him, playing on Luke's feelings of guilt. So he'd given him a house, a job, money. And then Jason had betrayed him by blackmailing his mother. A fact he hadn't discovered till he was in Indonesia going through some of her possessions. He'd threatened to very publicly expose her dead husband's indiscretions, which according to Jason, were many and damning. In doing so, he'd not only stain the memory and reputation of their father, but more importantly, would harm the image of the charity he'd founded. A charity that meant the world to Luke's mother.

Luke had told Meg none of the details. Maybe he should have because it sounded as though Jason had been playing on Meg's sympathies, too. All Luke had shared with her, when his death was looking like a distinct possibility, was that he didn't want to die knowing Jason, as his closest living relative, might benefit in any way.

"So how much help did you accept from him, and what did you mean by creepy?" The very thought of Jason anywhere near Meg was creepy. The man had the moral code of a hyena.

She shoved her hands deeper into her pockets. "He has an…unusual way about him. But he tried to be helpful. He gave me names of people and professionals for if I needed any work done, told me which restaurants were good. Things like that. But it was Mark who suggested the private investigator I used to try to track you down."

"You looked?"

"Of course I looked. But the investigator didn't turn up anything. So I went back there as soon as I got my visa renewed."

"To the island?"

"Yes." Sorrow clouded her eyes. "Where did you go? Where did everyone go?"

He hated the thought of her going back there. That it was for him made it even worse.

She'd left because the situation on the island had deteriorated rapidly into one of chaos and violence. She'd actually argued that she should stay with him, but the local staff had convinced her that they could care for him until the plane arrived to airlift him and a wounded islander to the nearest hospital for treatment.

"I don't know what happened to it, but the plane never

arrived. We gave it a day, but after fresh fighting broke out, we fled the village and then the island."

She nodded. "No one I spoke to had heard of you or any of the villagers we knew. At least they said they didn't. There was nothing left of the village itself. Or the school."

He heard the bleakness in her voice. It had made her sad, and it had made him angry. But there was nothing either of them could do about it now. The village had been caught in the middle of an escalating dispute linked to a decades-old conflict. "I know some of them got away. Were able to start afresh." That small truth was the best he could offer her.

She walked on, visibly subdued. Despite his earlier resolve to keep his distance, Luke slipped his arm around her shoulders and pulled her closer to him. The future would separate them, but they shared a past that no one else would understand. And he would offer her what comfort he could—the comfort of a friend—inadequate as it might be.

He still had questions, but now no longer seemed the time to ask them. They walked the rest of the loop in silence. His arm still about her shoulders. Her leaning subtly into him. He should let her go, but something about walking like this, with her, was deeply peaceful. He remembered that about her, a feeling of stillness and calm when she'd been the one nursing him.

The house, festooned with Christmassy boughs of greenery, came into view. In the eight years he'd lived here he'd never once decorated for Christmas.

He'd thought about putting up a tree one year, but if he put a tree up, then he'd have to buy ornaments. And, well, it just never happened. There was no point for a man living on his own. But this morning he'd noticed festive touches everywhere. Red bows on the uprights of the stairs, Christmas towels in the guest bathroom, a Christmas tree decorated in only white bows and white lights, simple but effective. "Where will you go?"

She stiffened. "That's not your problem or your concern. But," she drew in a deep breath that lifted her shoulders, "can I stay till Monday? Till my car's ready. It's at the mechanic's. That's why the committee meeting was here last night."

He stopped, forcing her to stop with him and looked at her. "Of course you can stay." He should be grateful. He'd been thinking two or three weeks, maybe a month, would be reasonable. But the thought of her leaving Monday was like having the rug pulled out from under his feet. Now that she wanted to go, he wanted to keep her near. Surely he ought to at least know his wife a little, if only so that he knew how she was likely to play it during their divorce.

Plus it would look strange to both his friends and hers if his wife left so soon. Ultimately, of course, they'd have to deal with it. But there was no hurry. "Stay as long as you need."

"Thank you," she said softly. "But Monday will be good." She gently turned down his offer. He'd wanted her gone, so he had no call to feel rebuffed. It had been like that back on the island. The conflicting feelings she evoked. The desire to have her near, the resenting of that desire and then the desire to have her back when she left. Turns out it wasn't contrariness caused by being bedridden.

She smiled at some hidden thought. She had the sweetest-looking lips. Eminently kissable. For all the admonishments he'd delivered to himself, he couldn't help wondering what she'd do if he kissed her again. No mistletoe, no audience.

She'd kissed him once. Back at the camp. The minister had left his bedside after marrying them. Darkness had fallen and Meg sat quietly by his side. She used to sometimes sit there and talk to him as he dozed, telling him stories from her childhood, as outside, unseen night insects sang.

The evening after their marriage she'd kept his hand in hers and Luke had lain there, eyes closed, trying to listen to what she said, but mainly just listening to the sound of her voice, the sound of home.

When he'd asked, after realizing it was something he should have asked first, she had talked about the boyfriend whose desertion had precipitated her trip to work with the foundation. About how she specialized in finding men who needed her for a time, emotionally, financially or physically, but then dumped her when the need had passed. Initially, she laughed at her own stories, but then, as she talked about her dreams of a family of her own, her voice changed, there was a catch to it, and then she stopped talking altogether. He opened his eyes to see a tear rolling down her cheek.

She tried for a smile. "Some wedding night, huh."

"Come here."

And she did. She moved from her chair to sit on the side of his bed.

"Closer."

She leaned down.

He brushed the tear away with his thumb and then slid his hand round to the back of her head, pulled her closer still and kissed her, slow and sweet, and he forgot about the pain and thought maybe he'd died and already gone to heaven.

She sat back up looking as shaken as he knew he'd feel if he wasn't so damn sick. Instead, he felt...a little better.

"Not bad for someone on death's doorstep." She tried to make light of what had just passed between them.

"Wait till I'm better." He winked. "I could make you forget all your sorrows."

"Is that a promise?"

"If you want it to be."

"Then get better. And I'll hold you to it."

"Now that's what I call an incentive."

It was the last time he'd been alone with her. The next day, she'd left on the boat that was to bring back supplies to replenish those raided from the island's medical facility.

But he wasn't sick now. He stopped walking and pulled her closer, let her see his intent. He read trepidation mixed with a little curiosity, a little anticipation in her gaze.

Beside them, Caesar growled deep and low. Meg stiffened and looked away. "Someone's here."

They rounded the side of the house to see a red Corvette driving away. Luke watched till Jason's car disappeared from sight before dropping his arm from Meg's shoulders and heading into the house. He hated what Jason had done to his mother, and hated the thought of him anywhere near Meg. He wanted the man out of his life for good.

The homemade wreath adorning his front door swung as he pulled the door open. Controlling his breathing, he stepped inside and held the door for Meg. She stood on the path at the base of the stairs watching him, her expression unreadable, her nose and cheeks pink from the cold.

Finally, looking straight past him, she climbed the stairs. He shut the door behind them and watched as she unwound her scarf. The peace and connection he'd found in her presence only minutes ago had vanished. She'd shut herself off from him.

He stood between her and the closet and took her scarf from her hands. "You don't understand."

"And I don't need to. Families are complicated. It's your business. It's nothing to do with me." She unzipped her jacket.

"You're my wife."

She stilled for a second, looking at her hands. "In name only."

"But still my wife." He didn't know why he was invoking the "wife" clause; he should be the last one reinforcing it. But he wanted her to understand.

"Don't tell me you aren't thinking about how soon you can divorce me, if you haven't started proceedings already."

"I haven't started proceedings."

"Yet. But you'll be at Mark's office first thing Monday morning?"

Luke said nothing. Meg looked up, met his gaze and nodded her understanding.

As she shrugged off her jacket, he moved to stand behind her, helped ease it from her shoulders and down her arms. He caught the scent of green apples but couldn't afford to be distracted by it. "You can't tell me you don't want to get divorced, too?" She turned, they were so close that he could encircle her with his arms. Hold her. Tell her everything. His wife in name only. Or they could not talk at all. He could taste her lips. Touch her skin. Feel her heat.

"Of course I want it, too."

Divorce, they were talking about divorcing.

"That's why I don't need to get involved in your personal life. Any more than I already am."

He hung up her jacket. "Any more than you are?"

She swallowed. "I'm living in your house. And I've made friends with some of your friends and their partners. I couldn't help it. When they learned about me, they wanted to meet me, to get to know me. They've been kind. I like them."

He nodded, gave her time to go on.

"Julie finally left her husband. She stayed here for a week when she first left. And Sally and Kurt are expecting their second child. She's due in three months. I said I'd help with babysitting when she went into hospital. And when she came out. You know how organized she is. Of course that might not be so easy now." She was talking fast, not meeting his gaze. "And I'm sorry. It just sort of happened." She looked up at him, apology in her eyes.

Just like he used to when he'd been sick, he'd gotten distracted by the soft cadence of her voice rather than focusing on the specifics of her words. The details of her supposed crime had washed over him. And today there had been the added distraction of his very real ability to do something about it. He could reach out, trail a finger down the softness of her cheek, touch it to those lips.

Desire stirred.

Three

Meg stepped back from Luke, the husband she didn't know, away from the warmth in his eyes. Warmth that had her thinking things she had no business thinking. She blamed the window. She'd come back from her walk with Caesar and looked up to see him standing at the wide picture window, wearing only boxers, his torso lean and sculpted, and a purely feminine thrill of appreciation had swept through her.

"I'm glad you found friends here, that you weren't alone," he said after a pause so long that she'd thought he hadn't been going to answer.

His softly spoken words disconcerted her. She didn't want to like him. At least not in the softening, melting way she could feel herself liking him. That was far more dangerous than the physical pull of attraction that she—and most likely the majority of the female population who came within his sphere—felt for him.

She'd agreed to marry him because he'd believed—rightly—that his death was a real possibility and it had seemed imperative to him that Jason not be able to inherit. She'd been prepared to do anything to ease his agitation.

But he hadn't died.

He was very much alive.

And watching her.

"But hopefully they have the good sense to stay away now that I'm back. All I want is peace and quiet."

Meg remembered the dinner. He might want peace and quiet but he wasn't going to get it. Not tonight, which was probably a good thing because Meg wasn't so sure she wanted to be alone with him.

"Show me round the house."

"I haven't changed anything. You don't need me to show you round it." Regardless of what he did or didn't need, *she* needed to put a little space between them. And she would—as soon as she'd told him about the dinner. Because the way they'd walked, with his arm around her, had felt so natural, and when he'd looked at her, he'd thought about kissing her and she'd wanted him to. It would feel so good, which would be all bad.

She was lonely. That was all. Her life had been on hold these last few months, but she was picking up the pieces again. She didn't need to lean on Luke.

Her work with the Maitland Foundation since she'd been back had been a welcome distraction.

"You've been having parties. That's a change."

"Do you mean last night? That was a final committee meeting."

"You put up Christmas decorations." He continued, not taking her opening to ask what the committee meeting was for. "That's a change. A bigger one than you know."

He flicked one of the red bows tied to the stair uprights. "I don't usually do Christmas."

It seemed a sad thing to say. She couldn't imagine not marking Christmas in some way. "That's not changing as much as adding something temporary." She was going to have to tell him about tonight.

The bow slipped and they both reached to catch it, hands tangling as they trapped the red velvet against the smooth wood of the post, halting its downward slide. For a second they stilled. His warm hand covered hers, pinning it with the bow beneath it.

He was close again. And again his proximity, his warmth and scent had her resolutions slipping. Meg slid her hand from beneath his, bringing the broad ribbon with it, and took a step back. With nerveless fingers she smoothed out the loops of the bow. From the kitchen she heard the strains of "All I Want for Christmas is You."

"Do you remember our promise?"

She glanced up to see him watching her closely, desire kindling in the depths of his eyes. He couldn't mean the promise her thoughts had leaped to. He must have meant their vows. "To love and honor? And only those vows because there was no time to write our own. 'In sickness and in health and to disinherit your brother and give me somewhere to live when I got back here.'"

A smile flickered and vanished. "That wasn't the promise I was talking about."

Oh. That promise. The one she'd secretly cherished in her darkest hours, something full of the possibility of tenderness and passion and the affirmation of life, and the one she'd now hoped he'd forgotten. "I don't think anything we said or did back then applies to the here and now."

"Some things transcend time and place," he said evenly. "And a promise is a promise."

Meg swallowed and tugged a little more at the bow.

"I sometimes think that promise was what I lived for," he said, almost to himself, "what kept me hanging on when I should have died waiting for the antibiotics to reach me."

She took another step back. His smile returned, knowing and tempting. "If it helped, then I'm glad of it." The bow came completely undone in her unsteady fingers.

He reached for the loose end, so that it became a connection between the two of them. "Did you ever think of it? Or did you forget about me altogether?"

She avoided the first of his two questions. "I didn't forget about you."

He pulled his end of the ribbon closer to him, bringing her hand with it. Then he lifted her hand, supported it with his own and with a sudden frown studied the ring that adorned her ring finger. "Our wedding ring?"

Meg shrugged, though with him cradling her fisted hand in his palm, nonchalance was the last thing she felt. "I had to have something. People were asking. I bought it over the internet so nobody would see me going to a jeweler's to get it."

"And this convinced them?" With the forefinger of his free hand he touched the simple thin gold band. "I would have chosen something a little more...expensive."

"Its importance is in what it symbolizes, not what it's worth. As I told your friends, this was all I wanted. Its simplicity and purity were the perfect representation of our relationship. Besides, I didn't want to spend a lot."

He straightened her fingers and the velvet ribbon whispered to the floor between them. "You paid for it yourself?"

"Of course." She tried to ease her hand free, but he held firm. "It wasn't much."

"I can tell. And our engagement ring?" He looked from her hand to her face. "Where's that?"

She shook her head. "We weren't able to get a suitable engagement ring. It was hard enough getting the wedding band, which we had brought over from another island." She filled him in on the details of the story she'd concocted for his friends. "You wanted us to choose the engagement ring once you came home, but I was going to argue against that. I like the band on its own."

"What else were we going to do once I came home?"

She swallowed. "Well, there was…our honeymoon. People asked about that." Which now that his return was real would be a divorce instead. Meg tugged at her hand and he allowed it to slide free.

Luke folded his arms across his chest and she could read nothing of his thoughts, how he felt about the stories she'd had to make up because she hadn't been able to tell people he married her out of desperation. It had seemed important that nobody, and especially the half brother he was so keen to disinherit, knew the true circumstances. "Do we know where we're going for that?"

"You wanted St. Moritz or Paris, but I wanted Easter Island."

"So we compromised?"

Meg allowed a small smile. "Um…no. We settled on Easter Island because you've been to St. Moritz and Paris before, but neither of us has been to Easter Island. And besides, we both wanted to see the statues." They had talked about the statues in one of their bedside conversations.

"I agreed they'd be amazing to see. Doesn't mean that's where I'd take my bride. I'd definitely go for a little more luxury. A little more hotel time, something a little more romantic."

"That's how people know how smitten you are with me."

"Smitten?"

"Hey." She smiled at his indignant expression. "It was my fantasy."

"Was it not supposed to be reality-based?"

"You're saying it's beyond the realms of possibility?" Her smile faded. Of course someone like him, a multi-millionaire, consistently named in most-eligible-bachelor lists, wouldn't really ever be interested in her, Meg Elliot, nurse. "Your friends believed it," she said in her defense, then frowned. "At least they said they did. They thought I was good for you."

"That's not what I meant. I was talking about realistic honeymoon destinations, not the reality of you and me together."

But Meg was on a roll. "They said I'm not like the women you've dated in the past—ones who don't challenge you emotionally, who let you shut yourself off from them. You must have finally realized what's important in life, must have trusted your ability to give and receive love."

"All my friends said that, or just Sally, who thinks one psych paper in college makes her Carl Jung?"

Meg hesitated, then sighed. "Mainly Sally," she finally admitted. But she'd so wanted to believe her, wife of one of Luke's friends, that she'd bought into her assessment.

Luke's sudden burst of laughter was the last thing she expected. "So, Easter Island, I can't wait to see those statues."

"It's not funny." He was still laughing at her. "I didn't

realize when I agreed to this pretence how complicated
it would get. I thought I'd come here and, well…I guess
I didn't really think about it at all. But there were people
with questions and expectations and I had to tell them
something."

"I'm sure you did the best you could."

"But you would have handled it better? What would
you have told them?"

"To mind their own damn business."

"You can't say that to people. And certainly not to
your friends."

"I can and I do. And friends are the ones who take it
the best."

"That's not my style."

"I guess I might have told them we were going somewhere private where I could keep the island promise
I made to my wife. That would have been almost as
effective at getting them to stop asking questions. They
know I don't make promises lightly."

And just like that any trace of levity left his face, but
he had to be joking still. Regardless, the sudden change
threw her off balance, swept away any sense she'd had
that she might be in control of their conversation.

To avoid the questioning intensity in his gaze and the
confusion it stirred, she stooped and picked up the ribbon
and began rolling it up. "That promise…" she said lightly,
trying to inject a touch of dismissive humor into her voice
"…it seems like it was a lifetime ago. Like we're not
those same two people." She had the ribbon half rolled
up when he caught the end. She studied their hands,
joined by a strip of red velvet. His large and tanned, hers
smaller and pale but thankfully steady.

"Look at me, Meg. And let me look at you." He still
sounded far too serious for her peace of mind. She could

almost imagine a trace of need in his voice. "I held your face in my mind for so long. I can't quite get enough of the real thing."

Which seemed the oddest thing to say about her. She had a talent for blending in and going unnoticed. She was the type of person people often forgot having met. Slowly, she looked up. He kept perfectly still as her gaze tracked over his torso, settling inevitably on his face, on the eyes that showed his wanting.

"I'm going to kiss you."

An even bigger surprise. She swallowed and shook her head. "That would be a bad idea." Because if he kissed her, she'd kiss him back, and then he'd know she wanted him. But while she knew she should just turn and walk away, she didn't. Her feet wouldn't listen to her head. He lifted the red velvet, drawing her hand up with it, and then he captured her wrist, raising her hand farther till he touched her fingertips to his jaw. A shiver passed through her and the velvet dropped again to the floor.

She used to touch his jaw like that when he was sick and weakened and feverish. But he was far from sick or weak now, and if anyone was feverish, it was her.

He turned his head and pressed a kiss to her palm. Warmth, heat, liquefied her bones. "I remembered your touch."

She couldn't stop herself, she cupped her palm around his jaw. So smooth now, so strong. He framed her face with his hands and lowered his head toward hers.

She had time to back away.

She stayed precisely where he was.

He kissed with exquisite gentleness. His lips were soft and seeking as though he was savoring the taste of her in the same way she savored the taste and feel of him. He kissed, drew back a fraction, kissed again, brushing his lips over hers. He angled his head, deepened the kiss, teased her teeth and tongue. Her mouth parted beneath his. His kiss was...beautiful. It was perfection. The way they fit so naturally together held an aching rightness. Made her feel that she'd been missing this, him, for so long.

She slid her arms around his waist and stepped into him. And still he kissed her, his fingers threading deeper into her hair.

Meg forgot all the reasons why this was a bad idea and lost herself in his kiss, in the simple joining. He gave of himself, made no demands, and because of that swept her away, a leaf delighting in the wind, flying for that brief time between tree and ground.

And for that brief time it was just him, just her, no past or future, just the now and this kiss, his lips against hers.

Too soon, but what had to be minutes later, he lifted his head, his hands still framed her face, his thumbs lazily stroked her cheeks.

"Remind me in what possible way that could have been a bad idea. I'm thinking it was one of the best, if not *the* best idea I've ever had."

She opened her mouth to speak and waited for her brain to provide the words.

He slid his hands over her shoulders, down her arms, till he held both her hands in his. And Meg knew she was in deep, deep trouble because all she could think was that she wanted him to kiss her again and then she wanted more. Much, much more.

The chiming of the doorbell broke through the sensory spell he wove. Her first reaction was disappointment. Her second, as sanity returned, was relief. That kiss could only have led to places they couldn't go, not without horribly complicating what was already a far-too-complicated situation, and not without threatening the safe cocoon she'd spun around her heart.

She started for the door.

"Leave it," he said.

But she'd remembered who it likely was. "Um... No. We can't." *We can't leave it and we can't go where you're thinking. Where I was thinking. Wanting.*

Luke looked from the broad cedar door to Meg. "You know who that is?"

Meg glanced at her watch. "Maybe." They were punctual, a little early even, which normally she'd rate as a good quality.

"So it's someone for you?"

"Not exactly."

"Whoever it is, send them away. I don't feel like company today."

"I can't do that."

"Because?"

The chimes rang softly through the house again. "Because I think it's the caterers."

His eyes narrowed on her. "Why are there caterers ringing my doorbell?"

"Because they'd like to come in?" She kept her tone hopeful and innocent.

"Meg?" His tone was anything but hopeful or innocent. She'd have said more suspicious and accusing.

"They have some setting up to do. For the dinner tonight." The doorbell rang again and was followed by an insistent knock.

"Open it. And then I think you better tell me what dinner they're setting up for."

Meg let the small army of caterers in, guided them through to the kitchen and took as long as she could showing them anything and everything she thought they might need to know. She didn't leave till it became obvious she was only getting in their way.

She went back to the entranceway where she'd left Luke, where he'd kissed her, but he wasn't there. The red bow was back in place on the post. She could look for him, but she'd doubtless see him soon enough. In the meantime, she had things she needed to do. Like run away before she started acting on three months' worth of daydreams.

In her—Luke's—bedroom she pulled a plain black suitcase from the wardrobe and dropped it onto her—his—bed and unzipped the lid. From the top dresser drawer she gathered her underwear and put it into the case. The second drawer contained Luke's clothes. She opened the third drawer and pulled out her T-shirts.

"What are you doing?"

She tensed at the sound of his voice and spun, her T-shirts clasped to her chest, to see him standing in the doorway. "Packing."

"You do have a knack for stating the obvious."

"We agreed I'd go as soon as you got back."

"And then we agreed Monday, because your car is at the mechanic's." Luke strolled across the room and positioned himself in front of the wide window that most days allowed forever views out over the lake. Today, ominous clouds hid the far, snow-capped mountains, restricting the view instead to the lake's edge. "What is it you're frightened of?"

"Nothing." And even though he wasn't looking at her, she clutched the T-shirts a little tighter, a flimsy barrier against his questions, his insight.

"Now, me, I'm frightened of you."

A ludicrous notion. "I don't think so. You hold all the

power here. Your house, your territory." Not to mention his looks, his wealth, her weakness for him.

"What scares me, Meg," he said to the window, "is the way I feel when I look at you. And the way those feelings intensify when you look back at me."

His words stilled her, made her want to hope. She covered the foolish, unlikely hope with glibness. "And I'll just bet you're a 'feel the fear and do it anyway' kind of guy."

"Sometimes," he said quietly. "Not always. Sometimes the fear is to protect us."

Meg placed the T-shirts on top of her underwear, spreading them so they hid the scraps of lace that were her secret indulgence. Plain, practical Meg liked pretty, sometimes even sexy, lingerie.

Luke crossed to the dresser. She'd divided the space on top in half. One-third, two-thirds, actually. A third for his things, a watch and a framed photo of his mother only needed so much space. The two-thirds on the right was littered with her things. Perfume, a pair of earrings, a scented candle and… "Don't touch that."

He turned with a curling photo in his hand. "This?"

"Yes," she sighed, "that."

"Why not?"

"I didn't mean don't touch it. You can have it. Throw it out if you like."

He lifted a questioning eyebrow.

"I needed something to show people when I went back to try to find you. Clearly, I don't need it anymore." The photo showed the two of them, Luke sitting up in bed, looking ill but still with a certain intensity to his gaze, and Meg perched beside him looking worried and pointing to something off camera. Their wedding photo.

She didn't even know why she'd left it out and on the dresser.

He was about to place the photo back where it had stood leaning against her perfume, when instead, he picked up the small crystal bottle and brought it to his nose. He closed his eyes and nodded. "Very Meg." Opening his eyes, he studied her. "Flowers and sweetness." Meg adjusted her T-shirts in the case.

"Tell me about this dinner the caterers in my kitchen are setting up for."

She opened her mouth to speak.

He held up a warning finger. "I just want the facts. No evasive answers. What party do you have planned for tonight?" He frowned. "And if you're planning a party, why are you packing as though you can't get out of here fast enough."

"There's a Christmas dinner for the Maitland Foundation here tonight. Most of the really big donors will be here. I haven't had all that much to do with the organization. I just agreed with Sally when she suggested that this house would be the perfect place for the dinner. And agreed with her that there was no reason it couldn't be here."

"She didn't tell you that she asks every year if she could have it here, and that every year I tell her no?"

Meg swallowed. Sally had told her she'd bear the blame if Luke got back before Christmas, but it didn't seem fair. "Actually, she did. But I couldn't see any reason not to have it here. You have a beautiful home. And it's so much more personal to have a dinner in a home than at a restaurant."

Luke blew out a heavy sigh. The hands at his sides had curled into fists. And for a few brief seconds he shut his eyes. Meg contemplated sneaking out. Too soon he opened them again, the silver sharp and intent. "So why are you packing now?"

"Now that you're back, I don't need to be here for it."

He crossed to the bed. Took everything out of her suitcase, dropped it onto the bedcover, then zipped the case shut. "Think again. If I have to be here for this dinner, then you most definitely do."

She unzipped the case and gathered up the pile of clothes. "No, I don't."

"These donors who are coming, they know I have a wife?"

"Yes, most of them," she said slowly, holding her clothes to her chest and hoping fervently that she'd covered her underwear with her T-shirts.

"Then they'll expect you to be here. The Maitland Foundation and its donors espouse strong family values. You could cost it thousands if you don't show, *Mrs.* Maitland."

"That's not fair."

"You're right, it's not." He smiled, devious and victorious. "I'll leave you to start getting ready." He stopped at the door and nodded at the clothes in her arms. "I'm sure the red will look fetching on you."

Meg glanced down. There were only two red items in her arms and neither of them was a T-shirt.

Four

Meg paused and wrapped her fingers around the polished wood of the banister. She'd made a point of staying out of the caterers'—and Luke's—way while she showered and dressed and put up her hair. But now she barely recognized the entranceway that she'd last seen just a few hours ago. Her homemade decorations were gone. The stairs were twined with ivy, among which nestled hundreds of glinting fairy lights. Below her, an enormous Christmas tree, topped with a star, glittered and sparkled in silver and gold in the entranceway, scenting the air with the fragrance of pine. Tall candelabra stood either side of the front door. The house was filled with the delicate notes of a string quartet playing Christmas music. It was as though someone had waved a wand and transformed the already graceful foyer into something magical.

Luke strode through the doors thrown wide from the

next room and had a foot on the bottom step before he looked up and stilled. A slow, knowing smile spread across his face. "I was just coming to get you. Our guests are starting to arrive, darling."

The wand must have touched Luke as well. Before now, she'd only ever seen him dressed casually. Even then, and even when ill, he'd looked striking, had an undeniable charisma. But now, in an elegant tuxedo, its cut and custom tailoring accentuating the breadth of his shoulders and his lean strength, he looked devastating. A surge of possessiveness and pride swept through her. This man was her husband.

She quashed both the possessiveness and the pride. She had no right to feel possessive of a man who wasn't in any way hers. And she had no right to the pride. He'd had to believe he was dying to offer marriage. Even so, he waited expectantly for her. And she couldn't quite calm the leap of her pulse.

Part of his attraction was the way when he looked at her she felt like he only saw her, only thought of her, as though she fascinated him every bit as much as he fascinated her.

Meg held a little tighter to the banister. She had only one dress suitable for a dinner like this. And it was red. Now Luke would think, and he'd be right, that she wore the red lace beneath it. Or worse, and he'd be wrong, that she wore it for him.

She descended the stairs. Wearing the demure but fitted dress and too-high heels, she was well out of her comfort zone. Or maybe it was his silver gaze steady on her that made her hyperaware of her every movement.

Tonight. She just had to get through tonight without succumbing to his pull. When she was away from him again she'd be fine, but when he was near, he scrambled her thought processes till she didn't know what she wanted, or till she wanted things she knew she oughtn't.

She stopped a step above him and finally, defiantly, met his gaze. And looked quickly away, her defiance doused. Heat. She'd read heat in his eyes. For her.

It was insane.

As insane as the heat of the response deep within her that his gaze had ignited.

He needed to get back out into the real world, remember the type of woman he was attracted to, the type of woman who belonged in his world, and stop playing games with her.

Except it didn't feel like a game.

She looked back at him, he waited, his hand extended. Trapped by his gaze, Meg swallowed and put her hand in his, felt his fingers fold around hers. And at that touch, that gentle, unerring connection, something shifted and changed, including Meg in this evening's magic.

Hope flickered. Might she be entitled to one enchanted evening?

She did her best to quash the thoughts. A childhood spent lost in books and fairy tales was now having the unwanted repercussions her grandmother had warned of.

Luke smiled, that same smile he had back up in her—his—bedroom as his fingers tightened around hers. "Let's go, Mrs. Maitland, we're having a party." His tone was light, teasing. Maybe she'd imagined the heat.

The living room was now decorated in silver and gold, with enough candles to keep them going for months if the power ever went out. Luke paused in the doorway and glanced up. Mistletoe hung from the door frame. In full view of those guests who'd already arrived, he planted a quick, hard kiss on her lips. Then he put his mouth close to her ear and whispered, "I knew you'd look good in red." His words and his warm breath on the bare skin of her neck sent a shiver through her.

Pretending she hadn't heard, hadn't been affected by his words or his kiss, Meg dredged up a bright, but possibly vacant, smile as guests approached.

"Wyatt, Martha, good to see you. You've met my wife, Meg?" Luke released her hand but rested it instead at the curve of her waist. She wasn't sure which disturbed her composure more.

He stayed by her side almost all evening as he worked the room with skill and ease. As head of Maitland Corporation, he left the running of the foundation to Blake, the director, but he spoke with knowledge and passion about the foundation's work. He talked to almost everyone, smiling and magnanimous, while at the same time ensuring Meg was included in conversations, asking her opinion on whatever topic came up. But he also took advantage of every opportunity, and created more than a few of his own, to touch her: to take her hand, or touch her arm, to curve his palm around her waist, to cup her shoulder. Once, claiming she had a crumb of pastry from a canapé on her cheek, he'd turned to her and brushed his thumb across her face, letting her see the heat in his eyes, making her want him.

And if he wasn't at her side, he was watching her, making her think about him, about their promise. The evening became an exquisite torture.

A bejeweled woman, who'd just promised the foundation a hefty donation, turned away, her parting words *See you both at the New Year's Eve cocktail party,* ringing in Meg's ears and Luke's gaze pinning her. He lifted two champagne flutes from the tray of a circulating waiter and passed one to Meg. He led her to a somewhat quiet corner of the room and she took a sip of the sparkling liquid.

"I was going to tell you about the cocktail party."

"Clearly I need to take a look at *our* social calendar and see what's expected of me. It's not in my house, is it?"

"No."

"Then I'll deal."

They watched the mingling crush. By then she'd be long gone. "I didn't realize you were such a people person."

"I'm not," he said softly. "But I know how to play the game." He turned his back on the room so that only she could see his face and hear his words. "The only person I'm thinking about is you and how good you look in red. And how good you'll look out of it."

His words, blatant and seductive, shocked her. How had they got to this point and, more importantly, how did she stop it? Because while she was certain it was all just a part of the "game" to him, if affected her differently, more deeply than he could know. "Don't do that."

"Do what?"

"What you've been doing all evening. I'm trying to concentrate, to listen to what people are saying and you're making me think…"

"Think what, Meg?" His low voice seemed to sink through her to her core. "About the things I might like to do with you? Because I've been thinking about my husbandly privileges."

She backed a little farther into the corner. "You're not really my husband." But he'd caught what she'd been thinking and she hated that he knew it. That she was that transparent. Because being married to someone carried connotations regardless of the reasons for the marriage.

He leaned closer. "That's the thing, Meg, I really am your husband. And you know it. And you think about it."

"Stop it, Luke. Please."

Something in her tone or her words stilled him. He backed off a little, easing her need to either reach for him or run from him. "If you want me to."

She nodded. "I do. Thank you." She was Meg. She wasn't allowed to want him. Not in the real world. She looked past him to see Sally approaching, glowing with the success of the evening so far.

"You two make a gorgeous couple." Sally kissed both Meg and Luke. "I'm so pleased you finally found a good woman, Luke, and had the sense to marry her. I foresee a long and happy union."

If only in my dreams. The line from the Christmas song popped into Meg's head. Now clearly wasn't the time to tell Sally that she was leaving and that Luke would be starting divorce proceedings as soon as possible.

Luke smiled and raised his glass to Sally, which could look like he was agreeing with her. It could, if you were Meg, also look like he was avoiding commenting on what she'd said.

She sat beside Luke for the dinner, ignoring the occasional press of his thigh against hers. He kept their topics of conversation neutral, his tone and his glances warm, only a degree or two more than friendly. For all of his subtle teasing foreplay earlier, he seemed, from the time of her request, to have switched off, or at least turned down the wattage on the sensual messages.

Whereas Meg had to fight to hide her feelings, and

fight to conceal the slow burning fuse of desire he'd lit and that now refused to be extinguished.

When the dinner was all but over, he sat back with his arm behind her and his hand curled around her arm, his thumb tracing lazy circles that sent heat spiraling through her. It was just a thumb. It shouldn't be able to do that.

She waited till he was deep in conversation with the man across the table before easing her chair back. Not deep enough, apparently. He dropped a firm hand to her thigh, anchoring her to her chair and looked at her, a knowing smile glinting in his eyes and touching his lips. "Oh, no, you don't. You're not running away now."

"I was just…" she could see him waiting for her excuse "…I'm not needed here," was the best she could come up with.

"I need you here."

She could almost wish that was true. He'd needed her once and married her because of it. That need had passed. He was back in his life, he was strong and healthy. His hand gentled on her thigh, but the heat of his palm burned through the silk of her dress, sizzled along her skin.

"I'm tired." She tried again, which was also true, although she didn't expect to sleep any more tonight than she had last night. Last night she'd been dealing mainly with the surprise of his sudden return. Tonight she'd be battling the strength of a desire that seemed to have flamed from nothing. Even though she realized now that the seeds had been sown and taken root back on the island. Then, she'd been able to ignore it, pretend it was something else. But she'd built fantasies around Luke. Fantasies she'd scarcely acknowledged.

She needed to leave. And not just this party. She

needed to leave this house, break the spell she was falling under. Already she was way too close to the precipice of stupidity.

"You can't leave," he said quietly, "because I have plans for you, Meg. Slow, sensuous plans." Holding her gaze, his hand inched farther up her thigh.

Lost. She was lost. The precipice rushed closer.

He wanted her and he knew she wanted him, knew what his touch was doing to her, how it heated her, and he knew she wanted more of it.

Luke pushed his chair back. Claiming jet lag, he excused them both.

In the entranceway, he shut the double doors behind them, muting the sounds of music and conversation. Illuminated only by flickering candles and fairy lights, he murmured, "Mistletoe," and then pulled her to him and kissed her. Meg welcomed the press of his hard body against hers, reveled in the taste of him. The man she'd married. His mouth and lips and tongue teased and explored and seduced. Already, she knew the way their mouths fit together, knew the scent of him. He gripped her waist, slid his hands to cup her behind, she answered his pull with an involuntary rocking of her hips.

He shuddered in her arms and broke the kiss to rest his forehead against hers, breathing as heavily as she was. "I made you a promise, Meg. Will you let me keep it?"

Five

Meg nodded her agreement, the small movement moving both their heads. Reaching up, Luke pulled the mistletoe free, then led her past the Christmas tree slowing only enough to brush his lips across hers. Once, and then again. Light and shadows danced across his face.

They entered a hallway and he shut the door behind them, once again turning her, pressing her up against it as he kissed her, one hand holding the mistletoe above them, the other sliding up beneath her dress over nylon, encountering bare skin at the top of her thigh.

The hand stilled, the kiss stopped and the mistletoe dropped to the floor.

Luke drew back. "Stockings?" he asked, his voice hoarse but his fingers still burning against her skin.

Meg shrugged, her throat suddenly too dry for words. She hadn't meant the stockings for him; she preferred them to pantyhose, but she also liked their risqué-ness, as she liked her lacy lingerie. It was supposed to be her *secret* weakness.

"Pretty, quiet, Nurse Meg. I knew there was more to you than met the eye. Be very, very grateful I didn't know that till now." He took a step back from her. "Show me."

She hesitated. She was no lingerie model.

"Show me," he insisted again, his voice a command as though she were a siren, as though she, Meg Elliot, tempted him to danger.

"I can't." Shyness warred with a budding sense of power. "Not here. Someone could come this way."

Luke grasped her hand and tugged her down the hallway and into the first door they came to, shutting it behind them. Meg took a few steps into the library with its walls of books and its two-seater couch. She turned back to see Luke leaning against the door, watching her. "Show me."

Somewhere in the last hour she'd stopped pretending to herself that she didn't desire him, hadn't always recognized that something in him called to her. One night with her husband. She was entitled to that much, wasn't she?

Slowly, her hands against her thighs, she walked her fingers to gather up the fabric of her dress, lifting it higher till the tops of her stockings were just visible, a stark line against her pale skin. She opened her hands and let the fabric fall back into place.

Luke stood utterly still. Never had she seen such naked desire in a man's eyes. And it was all for her.

He closed the gap between them and holding her gaze ran both hands beneath her dress and up the outside of her thighs till his palms cupped the strip of skin between black nylon and red lace. His eyelids dropped lower and he drew in a deep, shuddering breath as his hands slid farther around, cupping and pulling her against him.

And then he kissed her, the way only he ever had, fitting his mouth perfectly to hers, slowly, sweetly, joining them seamlessly and with just his kiss transporting her, promising her pleasure. Heat and urgency and need that inflamed her with reciprocal need. Hooking his thumbs over the edge of her panties, he slid them down her legs and she stepped out of them—a scrap of lace on the dark wood flooring.

Large, warm hands skimmed back up her thighs, passing the tops of her stockings till they rested on bare skin.

She'd drunk only a few sips of champagne throughout the evening; the intoxication that governed her now was fueled by desire. Meg tugged the hem of his shirt free, sliding her own hands against the heat of him. She pulled his bow tie undone, and with frantic fingers worked at the buttons of his finely pleated shirt till she could push apart the sides and touch her palms, her fingers, to the strength and contours of his torso. She eased his shirt back from his shoulders. A raised scar ran across his right shoulder. The gash that had started the chain of events that led to now. She touched her lips to his shoulder, grateful for the first time for that injury.

Beneath her fingertips lay the heated silk of skin over hard, contoured muscle, the light abrasion of hair, she felt his deeply indrawn breath and the rapid beat of his heart, knew it matched her own.

He cupped his hand between her legs, slid a finger through her folds, found her wet for him. Silver eyes darkened to pewter. "Tell me what you want, Meg."

No one had ever asked her that. And the answer was

both complicated and blindingly simple. "I want you. Now."

He led her to the couch, sat and pulled her down on top of him, her knees straddling his thighs, she pressed her center against the hardness of him. Luke kissed her lips, her throat, her shoulder. He pushed the skirt of her dress up so he could freely touch the skin that seemed to so delight him. Enthralling her in the process.

He slipped the clips from her hair so that it tumbled loose around her shoulders. Finding the zipper at the back of her dress, he slid it down, peeled the dress from her so that it was now no more than a silken red pool of fabric around her waist.

"Show me how you like to be touched. I want to give you pleasure."

Already he was. So much more pleasure than she'd ever known. Warm hands and warmer lips skimmed over every inch, every curve and dip of bare and lace-covered skin, caressing and teasing, adding fuel to the already-burning flames, till she writhed with need. She covered his hands with hers as he cupped her breasts and her head fell back.

For now, he was her husband. And she wanted him. Needed him. Hard and deep within her.

For now.

"Condom?" Please, please let him have one because heaven knew what she'd do if he didn't.

He nodded, pulling a foil square from his pocket as she reached for his zipper and freed the straining length of him. Waiting just long enough for him to cover himself, she slid down onto the length of him, bringing him home, shuddering with pleasure as he stretched and filled her.

His gaze locked with hers, intent and powerful, as

she rocked against him, with him, over him. Passion turned his eyes storm-dark. Her fingers dug into his shoulders as his hands gripped her hips and they found a building rhythm of their own. Clamoring need and desperate desire drove them higher and faster till sensation, the effervescence of champagne bubbles, filled and overwhelmed her. She cried her arching completion moments before he drove his release home.

Meg fell forward, resting her head on the top of his and he snaked his arms around her waist and held her to him, his ear to her thudding heart. When he'd promised to make her forget her sorrows, she hadn't realized he'd make her forget her very self. That in his arms she would forget her inhibitions and become the woman she imagined she saw in his eyes.

The silence and stillness of the room stole over them as her heartbeat slowed and her gasping breath eased.

What now? Too soon the taunting inner voice asked. What now, indeed. She had no idea, no answer. Her mind still reeled from the power and passion of their lovemaking. She pulled away from Luke, and his clasp loosened. She slipped her arms back into the sleeves of her dress. He helped ease the fabric up over her shoulders, planting a kiss between her breasts the moment before the spot was covered. She eased out of his lap and Luke stood, too.

Not meeting his gaze, she turned and searched for her panties. She bent to pick them up, but they were snatched out of her reach before she touched them. He slipped them into his pocket.

Wordlessly, they walked to the library door. She reached for the handle, but he covered her hand with his. And when she looked at him, he kissed her, gentle and lingering. They turned the handle together and stepped

out into the hallway. When she would have headed the
way they had come he shook his head, and with a firm
grip on her hand led her farther down the hallway. He
stopped at the third door. The guest room. His room.

His seeking gaze searched her face. "This time I want
you naked and beneath me."

Meg caught her bottom lip with her teeth. Apparently
finding what he sought, Luke opened the door and pulled
her with him into the darkened room, whispering, "Never
let it be said that I didn't utterly satisfy my wife."

Meg woke in her husband's bed, her head resting in
the hollow of his shoulder, her arm draped over his chest,
her legs entwined with his.

He'd kept his promise and given her so much more.

Slowly, carefully, she disentangled herself and eased
from the bed. He didn't so much as stir.

As she slipped back into her dress and gathered up
her discarded stockings and shoes, she paused by the
wide window. They'd slept with the curtains open and
overnight a light snow had fallen, dusting the trees and
boulders on the lake shore. The sight was so beautiful
that it made her heart ache. Soon she'd be gone from here.
She'd stepped onto a stage and played her part. But the
time for her exit was drawing inexorably closer.

Feeling like an intruder, she slunk back through the
still house. Bundling up against the cold, she took Caesar
for his morning walk along the shore, tossing his stick
repeatedly. Tempted by beauty's promise of stillness and
serenity, she walked out to the end of the jetty and looked
over the lake. The mountains on the far side were still
obscured by heavy cloud.

At the sound of footsteps, she turned, a leap in her
pulse. Not Luke but Jason. Her heart sank and she real-

ized she'd hoped, wanted, it to be Luke. Wanted to see the man she'd made love to last night. Wanted to see his face and at the same time was afraid to. In the light of day would there be any of last night's tenderness and connection, or would it be regret and distance she saw there?

"I thought I saw someone down here." Jason smiled, warmth in his voice. He looked a little like Luke. Similar build and coloring but his watery-blue eyes were always moving, scanning the surroundings.

Meg smiled back, but doubts gnawed at her. What had Jason done to cause Luke to dislike him so intensely? Intensely enough that he would rather marry her than have his half brother inherit from him.

"So are the rumors true? Has my brother come home?"

Half brother. Meg nearly said that out loud. Luke was always careful to draw the distinction. "Yes."

Jason's smile wavered and he glanced over his shoulder at the house. Was that anxiety in his question? Jason had always seemed eager for Luke's return.

"I was just going back inside. Come in. He's probably up by now." Meg walked back along the jetty. Jason fell into step beside her.

"I'm on my way to meet someone and I want to go before there's any more snow. I haven't got time to stop. I'll call in later."

She shrugged. "I'll let him know to expect you."

"And let him know…"

She waited for him to finish.

"Nothing," he finally said. "Just…put in a good word for me, will you?" She walked round to the front of the house with him. As he drove away, she climbed the stairs.

The front door swung open. Luke, in jeans and bare feet, pulled an olive-green T-shirt over his head. He tugged the hem of the shirt over the plane of his stomach and looked past Meg. Jason's red Corvette disappeared around a bend in the road, leaving it empty and still. "Damn." Luke's gaze came back to her. "How long was he here and what did he want?"

"Not long and to know if you were home." Meg stepped past Luke and into the house. The Christmas tree dominated the entranceway. They'd kissed here last night. Her face heated with the recollections of where that had led to.

Luke's hand wrapped around her wrist, stopping her when she would have walked away, turning her back to face him. "What did you tell him?"

"I told him that yes, you were home."

"What else?"

Meg tugged her hand free. "Ask him yourself. I don't want to be a pawn in your petty squabbles."

"They're not petty."

"No, I suppose not." For all that she hadn't known Luke long, she knew him well enough to be certain of that. "But I still don't want to be caught in the middle of whatever it is. I think Jason really did try to help me while you were gone."

"If he did, it was for his own reasons." The creases in his brow deepened. "He blackmailed my mother."

A woman who'd devoted her life to others. A year after her death, the villagers still spoke of her with love, talked about her compassion and understanding and her ability to get things done. They'd probably still be talking about her a decade from now. And Jason had blackmailed her? "No." He wouldn't have, would he?

"Right up until her death. I didn't find out till I went through her papers in Indonesia."

"I remember your saying you'd discovered something about him. You were so angry."

"Still am."

As Meg repositioned a gold bauble on the tree, she could just make out his distorted reflection in its surface. "What are you going to do about it?"

"I haven't made a final decision. I want to talk to him first. Confront him with it."

"Will you bring charges?" She turned back to him.

Grimness tightened his mouth. A mouth that could give such pleasure. "Most likely. After I strip him of the car, the house and the job I gave him."

"Oh."

"Don't play the disappointed-in-me card, Meg. The man was blackmailing my mother. I owe it to her."

"You're right, and I'm not disappointed."

"But?"

"I just wondered if that was your only option."

"Unless you can suggest a better one, one that does justice to my mother?"

As Meg shook her head, he slid his phone from the pocket of his jeans, punched in a number. "Jason. You should have stuck around." Did Jason hear the command in the quietly spoken sentence? Meg tuned out the short conversation as she walked away. Luke caught up with her in the kitchen as she was pouring two coffees. "He'll be back later today."

She passed him a mug. As she lifted hers to her nose to inhale the fragrance, the ring on her finger caught her eye. The dinner was over, there was no need for her to wear it any longer. Putting down her coffee, she twisted the simple gold band from her finger and held it out to him.

He looked at her hand but didn't reach for the ring and a glimmer of a smile touched his lips. "You can't give it back to me. I never gave it to you in the first place."

Oh. Right. So much for that gesture. Feeling like a fool, she went to slip the ring into her pocket. He did reach for her then. He picked up her left hand and slid the ring back into place. "But leave it there for now. I didn't want to make you a pawn, Meg. I wanted to give you something."

"And to stop Jason getting anything."

"Mainly that," he agreed. "And you know what else?"

"What?"

"This isn't how I planned on starting this morning."

She didn't want to think about what he might mean by that. There were a number of possibilities. All of the ones that sprang to her mind were unwise.

He tugged her closer, pressed a soft, beguiling kiss to her lips. Very unwise.

"Good morning," he said with a smile once he'd pulled away, his gaze locking on to hers.

All of her tension had melted with just that one kiss. It was a masterful tactic, a potent secret weapon in his arsenal. "Good morning." *Kiss me again.*

But he didn't. "Have you had breakfast? Or is it lunch-time already again?"

"Breakfast, and no, I haven't eaten. But Luke, I think I should go."

She watched his face, his eyes, but couldn't read his reaction. "Eat first," he finally said.

Not, *No, don't go, Meg,* which she would have been foolish to expect. Sometimes, though, she was foolish. Last night being the most recent example. Making love to a man she had no future with. Letting herself love him, even just a little.

In the kitchen, he had her sit on a stool at the breakfast bar while he got out a pan and bacon and eggs. "How did you learn to cook?" No man had ever cooked for her.

He passed her a mug of coffee. "Mom got heavily into her charity work from an early age. She wasn't always around a lot. And when I was a teenager I went through several years of being constantly hungry. Appetite's a great motivator. It's not like I can produce a gourmet meal or anything, but I can do the basics. You want a filling, sustaining meal after or before a day's snow skiing or water skiing? I'm your man."

I'm your man? The expression was depressingly appealing. As was the man himself.

Within a few minutes he'd carried two plates of eggs and crispy bacon to the small oak table in the breakfast nook. He sat at a right angle to her and they ate in a silence that would have been restful were it not for Meg's regret and quiet despair about how soon this was ending.

Beyond the window, snow flakes began to drift and swirl.

She hadn't heard a weather report in days, but Jason had spoken as though more snow was expected. "Thank you." She stood from the table. "Now I should go." She had to end it. The sooner the better. Drawn-out goodbyes were too hard, too painful.

"I thought your car was at the mechanic's till tomorrow."

That was her problem. "It is." She caught her bottom lip in her teeth. "You could take me to Sally's?"

Silver eyes assessed her. "Is that what you want?"

No, I want you to ask me to stay. To see where this

thing we have leads. Unless this thing we have is all in my head. "Yes, it's what I want."

"Because from what I know of you, the things you've told me, the things I've seen, you don't always consult your own needs."

Meg said nothing. Was she that transparent? She did put other people's needs ahead of her own. That was how she'd been brought up. That was what she was supposed to do, wasn't it?

"You've called her?" he asked after a pause.

"Not yet." But she would, and could only hope that Sally kept her questions to herself. For her months here she'd pretended she'd had a real marriage. Now, two days after her husband's return, she was seeking sanctuary at her friend's place. But fortunately, in those two months, Sally truly had become a friend.

"What does staying at Sally's achieve?"

Couldn't he just let it go? She sighed and tried to keep her voice neutral. "Distance. Perspective. It gives you your home and your life back." But mainly, it would stop her doing dumb things like watching his hands as he held his fork or his cup and remembering the feel of those hands on her.

Luke looked toward the window but said nothing.

Meg paused at the doorway. "I'll need an hour to gather up all my things from around the house and finish packing."

He gave a single abrupt nod and she left the room. It was easy enough to pack up her clothes and belongings from the master bedroom, but she took her time, folding slowly, uncharacteristically uncertain about how best to pack her bags. In the wardrobe, she let herself touch Luke's suits, his sweaters. Beside the bed, she straightened the fishing magazine and the book that she'd left all this time on the bedside table. She'd read the book—a thriller—her first month here. Imagining a connection with him as she did so. Her fingers turning the same pages his had.

She lingered in front of the wide window. Its view over the lake had always brought her a measure of serenity. It didn't today. Today, the dark turbulent sky matched the oppression she felt.

She finished in the bedroom but needed to check the rest of the rooms. Over the months she'd lived here, she'd managed to spread herself and her bits and pieces throughout the house. She'd have to do a room-by-room search.

At the door to the library, she paused, not sure she wanted to face the scene of last night's…encounter. She toyed with the idea of just buying a new book to replace the half read one she'd left in there, then decided she was being ridiculous. She was a grown woman, for goodness' sake. She pushed open the door and stepped inside.

Luke sat on the couch, a sheaf of hand-written papers on his lap, his long denim-clad legs stretched out and crossed at the ankles. He looked up as she entered and the memories came flooding back.

Memories of sights; shadows and contours, and scents; his shampoo, his sweat, the essence of Luke himself and sensation; frantic hands, warm lips on skin, desperate longing and utter completion filled her mind. Images of her own reckless abandon.

"I just," she cleared her throat, "came to get my book." She pointed at the book on the small table beside him. He watched her silently as she dashed forward to snatch it up and backed out of the room.

As she shut the door behind her again, she thought she heard him speak. A short phrase, too indistinct for her to make out. *Show me.* She was imagining things. Nothing to show. No stockings today, no red lace. White and a little lacy, with a small bow between her breasts. But mainly plain. That's who she really was. But for a few forbidden seconds she imagined the things she could wear for him if— She cut off her own thoughts. No ifs. No maybes. They'd had an agreement. She'd lived up to her part of it. And now she was going. Last night was…a bonus. Such an inadequate word. A night's insight into a world of possibilities, of pleasure and promise and wholeness.

Ten minutes later he found her on the stairway, strode up to meet her and took her case from her hand. He carried it down, set it by the Christmas tree in the entrance. "There's more?"

"One."

She followed him up to the bedroom. Her second case, bulging and heavy, sat at the base of the bed. He looked about the room, his gaze sweeping from the bed to her face. "I'll think of you when I'm sleeping in here."

"Don't, Luke."

"Don't think of you when I'm sleeping in here? Or don't tell you that I will?"

"Don't…tell me." It was only fair that he think of her; she'd thought of him often enough as she'd lain there, and knew she would think of him still wherever she went next. For a time at least. But time healed all, dulled memories and yearnings. Eventually she'd forget him. Forget last night. Move on. She had to.

"I spoke to Mark this morning."

The simple statement doused the recollections. Mark was his attorney as well as his friend. "And?"

"And he's coming round tomorrow morning. But he

said, whatever we do, we shouldn't sleep together." His lips twitched.

How could he think this was funny? But his amusement called a response from her, a spark of un-Meg-like mischief. Mark would surely be appalled at how incautious their actions had been. "Did you tell him?"

Luke shook his head. "Didn't want to spoil his weekend. I'll tell him tomorrow."

"It won't make a difference, you know." She wanted Luke to know that. "I don't want anything from you. I never did. The fact that we slept together doesn't change that."

"Nothing, Meg?" He picked up her case as though it was weightless. "When you have money, it seems everyone wants something from you. It's hard to believe that there are people who really don't."

Maybe he wouldn't truly believe that till she walked away from him.

"Even my mother. She only approved of me and what I did because it meant I could donate money to her causes. And maybe she was right."

"That wasn't the only reason she approved of you. She loved you."

"I'm sure she did." He spoke without conviction.

"She couldn't not have." Meg spoke with more vehemence than she'd meant to. She half loved him herself and she'd known him only a whisper of time.

Luke's eyebrows lifted. And Meg regretted the intensity of her words. Did they reveal too much? Too much of what? She couldn't even say herself. Her feelings, her heart, were galloping ahead to places her mind knew they shouldn't. They'd passed like, and attraction, passed fascination and warmth, were mired in enthrallment, a deep drugging spell of connection and wanting and rightness. But she wouldn't let it be anything more than that. It was a spell that could, and would have to, be broken. Because she was leaving.

That was what they'd agreed.

Six

Luke carried Meg's suitcase downstairs, set it beside the first and said what he'd known for the last hour. "We're going to have to wait till the snow stops and the roads are cleared." She followed his gaze through the panes of glass bordering the door. Snow had blanketed the pines and the ground outside in white and was still falling.

He didn't know what to expect. Frustration that she couldn't get away, as she so clearly wanted to, or resignation that she was stuck here with him for longer still? He didn't expect her to step toward the door and place her fingertips on the glass, soft wonderment in her expression. "I grew up in southern California. It never snowed." She glanced at him. "It's so beautiful," she said, turning back to the window.

As she was, beautiful and serene and unspoiled, like the snow outside.

And always able to find a silver lining.

"It might be. But it's no good for driving in." He was deliberately brusque because it beat the hell out of getting sappy, of letting the way she affected him on so many levels show. They'd made love last night, but she was going this morning. It was for the best. Too much time with her was blurring the lines between what he ought to do, send her off so that she could find someone less jaded, someone who shared her optimism and her dreams, and what he wanted to do, take her back upstairs to his bed, make her his, hope a winter-long blizzard moved in.

He needed to find some kind of middle ground. "Let's go for a walk."

Her slow smile of pleasure and approval warmed him. Or maybe all she felt was relief at not being trapped indoors with him. He handed her her coat from the closet. "There are so many things we'll never do together. But we've got this day, whether we like it or not."

She'd be gone soon enough. A walk in the snow couldn't hurt. Layers and layers of clothing. And it was surely better than being inside with her with little to do except be ambushed by thoughts of making love to her again, sinking into her heat, of watching a different kind of wonderment on her face, of seeing her ecstasy. Which was how he'd spent the morning. Staying out of her way but acutely aware of her.

She was her own kind of delirium. He could no longer pretend his reaction to her was a product of fever, and honesty compelled him to admit that something about her had called to him well before his infection had become serious. The attraction of innocence, of her optimism? Wanting to drench himself in her aura. *Snap out of it.* He shoved his arms into his coat, hands into gloves and his feet into snow boots and stood apart from her, not so much as looking at her, while he listened to her movements, the rustle of clothing, the zipper on her jacket sliding up, a soft stomp as she pushed her feet into boots.

He opened the door and stepped outside, breathed deeply of the Meg-free air. The door closed behind him. Her shoulder nestled against his. Her scent assailed him. The scent he'd reveled in last night.

She walked ahead, tripping lightly down the steps, her footsteps crunching through snow as she skipped ahead, her brightly colored Sherpa hat bobbing with her footsteps, the tassels by her ears swinging like braids. Already she was committed to an idea that was nothing more than an off-the-cuff suggestion to find a way through the situation. Luke followed, gloved hands in his pockets, his step measured and slow. She stopped, flung her arms wide, tipped her face skyward and spun in a slow circle, embracing the day. Already her nose and cheeks were pink. He wanted to kiss her. Heaven help him. He wanted to kiss those cheeks, those eyes, those lips. "Help me make a snowman." She crouched down, gathered a ball of snow and began rolling it.

She'd make a great mother. Not something he'd ever thought before about the women he'd been involved with. She had so much of the carefree spirit of a child within her. And yet she'd seen hardship, she'd been confronted with it daily in Indonesia. Seen it and chosen to keep the flame of optimism alight within her. He crouched, too, began rolling a second snowball. He couldn't remember the last time he'd done this, certainly not since he was a child. He stacked his snowball on top of the larger one she'd rolled and began rolling a third for the head.

"Carrot," she announced, "for the nose. And I don't suppose you have buttons?"

He shook his head.

She headed back to the house. "I'll find something."

Luke was settling the head in place when Meg came hurrying back with a carrot and two plums. She pressed the carrot and fruit into place, one of the plums shedding a single purple tear. Then she wrapped her scarf around the snowman's neck and pulled a camera from her pocket. "Stand by Frosty."

"Frosty?"

"It's almost Christmas. What else are we supposed to call him?"

He reached for the camera. "You stand by...Frosty. I'll take your picture."

She shook her head and the light in her eyes dimmed just a little. "I'd like one of you."

To remember him by? "For that matter, I'd like one of you." To remember her by. Even though he had the feeling his problem was going to be in trying to forget her.

She shrugged and stood by the snowman. "Come stand with us. My arm is just long enough to take a picture of us both."

He stood at her side and taking a glove off, eased the camera from her hand. "My arm's longer." She pressed up against him and without thinking, he slid his free arm around her shoulders, pulled her closer. The thinking occurred too late, when he inhaled the fragrance of her shampoo. "On three. One. Two. Three." The shutter clicked.

"One more," she said. "Just in case."

"On three again." This time on three, as the shutter clicked she wriggled in his hold and planted a quick kiss on his cheek.

"Let me see it," she said as though she hadn't just done

that—kissed him as though it was a perfectly ordinary thing to do. Which, perhaps with someone else it would be, but from Meg it hadn't felt ordinary. It had felt like a gift.

Refusing to be distracted, he adjusted the setting to replay and, not looking at the picture, passed her the camera. What he did look at was her. Her breath coming in small misty puffs. Her cheeks and nose getting redder still with the cold. The lips that had moments ago touched his face. So much for not getting distracted.

He dropped all pretence of resolution and cupped a hand to one rosy cheek. Meg looked up, a smile playing about her lips. The smile dimmed and her lips parted as she read his intent. Using his teeth he pulled his other glove off, let it fall to the snow so that he could frame her face with both his hands. Skin against skin.

Slowly, he lowered his head and kissed her.

Properly.

If they only had this day left, if he only had a finite and too-limited number of kisses left, then he wasn't going to let her waste them on his cheek.

The warmth of her mouth was an erotic contrast to the chill of her lips. Her heat, as his tongue teased and tasted, swamped him. She wrapped her arms around his waist and kissed him back, softened against him. Pure Meg. Laughter and depth, temptation and innocence. His past, his present and his— Just his past and his present. That's all it would be.

He kissed her still, widening his stance so that he could fit her more closely against him. Kissing her out here was safe. Layers of clothing and a bitter chill to prevent his taking any of them off. But the temptation was so great that he'd likely stay out till they both froze just for the pleasure of feeling her pliant mouth beneath his, her warmth and sweetness, her eagerness.

It was Meg who broke the kiss, leaning back, her arms looped around his waist so that her hips pressed a little more firmly against his. "I don't think we should."

He'd think a little more clearly if it wasn't for those hips. He knew all the reasons why she was right. This was ending. And it needed to end cleanly. As cleanly as was possible given what had already passed between them. He didn't want to hurt her. "You're right. But just one more." He waited for her smile, waited till the indecision in her eyes was swept away by agreement and the flare of hunger as she abandoned reason and caution and lifted her face to his. Meg. His wife. So quick to respond to him. Something primal stirred. More than lust. He chose not to examine it, let desire and pure pleasure take the upper hand.

They were both breathing heavily, their breaths mingling in the air, by the time she again pulled away. And this time she broke all contact, stepping away from his touch, turning to adjust the snowman's carrot nose. "We should go in."

And this time he knew better than to disagree. Because despite what he'd thought, kissing her out here wasn't safe. Far from it. Kissing the way they had been spoke too openly of more, of picking up where they'd left off last night. Of his falling into her heat. Of staying there.

"Besides, I'm cold." Her cheeks were flushed.

Luke lifted her hand, pulled a glove off and enclosed her fingers in his. He tucked her hand against his side as he led her back to the house.

Inside again, he hung up their coats. He didn't look at her cases by the front door as he led her toward the living room, knew a moment's hesitation as they passed the Christmas tree, he wouldn't kiss her inside, knew another moment as they passed the stairs, the stairs he wouldn't lead her up to his bedroom. Finally in the relative sanctuary of the living room, he lit the fire. "Stand here. Warm yourself."

Unquestioning and not meeting his gaze, she held her hands out to the flames.

Luke left the room, returned in five minutes carrying two cups of cocoa. He didn't know why looking after her gave him such pleasure and satisfaction, but it did. She stood exactly where he'd left her, staring into the flames.

"You're warm enough?" He handed her a cup of cocoa and she nodded as she took it, seemingly intrigued by the marshmallows floating on the top.

"What now?" she asked.

Almost all of the ideas that sprang to mind were unwise. "I have a suggestion."

Her gaze lifted and narrowed on him.

"Not that." He laughed. Because if he didn't laugh he'd take the assumption as an invitation. "Not that the idea doesn't have merit." A slow blush crept up her face. "I'm suggesting a movie." She quickly covered the flash of disappointment in her gaze. But the flash had pleased the unwise part of him. Like her, he covered the reaction. He slid a movie into the player, picked up the remote. "The snow's stopped. Soon enough the roads will be cleared and you'll leave." He led her to the couch and sat close beside her, pulling the broad coffee table closer so that he could rest his feet on it. She watched him, waiting for him to continue. He settled into the soft black leather of the couch, pulled her back with him and tried to explain his reasoning. "I never intended to marry. Never thought I would. I don't need other people the way some do.

I'm content on my own." He slipped an arm around her shoulders. "So this might be it. My only chance to spend time with my wife. To experience married life. We can be like an old couple who have comfortable routines they've settled into over a lifetime of being together. Cocoa and a movie on a snowy afternoon. We'll argue over chick flick or action movie." He picked up the remote, pointed it at the TV and the screen flickered to life. "Action movie will win because we watched your chick flick last week."

As the opening credits rolled and on-screen a car wound its way up a rocky mountainside at night, she nestled a little closer and stretched her legs out alongside his, resting her small feet, in their red socks, beside his.

They were an hour into the movie which had managed to capture only a portion of his awareness away from her, when Caesar started barking. Moments later the doorbell chimed. Luke glanced at his watch, his mood darkening. He stood. "You keep watching. I just have to deal with this."

She reached for the remote, located the Pause button. "I'll wait."

"I'm not sure how long this will take. Depends on how much of a fuss he makes."

"He? Jason?"

Luke nodded, resenting this intrusion, the sullying of his afternoon with her. But he needed to deal with it. He'd been thinking about their earlier conversation, about finding a way to deal with Jason that did justice to his mother.

"I'll wait," she said, looking away from him as she settled back into the cushioning leather, looking small and stoic, expecting better of him than he was prepared to give. On-screen, the hero was frozen with a gun pressed to the villain's temple, his eyes bleak.

Seven

Seconds after Luke strode from the room, the sound of voices, muted but clipped, reached Meg, then faded as they headed to Luke's office along the hallway. She made a bowl of popcorn, set it on the coffee table and then crossed to the wide windows. Outside, Frosty stood a lonely sentinel on the lawn, Meg's scarf loose about his neck, his eyes dark and desolate. For a time she heard nothing. Then shouting. She crossed to the open living room door, her fingers gripping the door frame, hesitant.

Only one man was shouting. Jason. She couldn't hear Luke at all.

She was still standing there, distressed by the anger she heard and wondering whether there was anything she could do to help, when the voice quieted. A minute later, Jason stormed out of Luke's office, slamming the door behind him. He stalked along the hallway toward her.

"Will you be okay?"

Jason looked up, a dark dislike glittered in his eyes. "Don't pretend you care."

"I'm not pretending."

His step slowed. "Then call your husband off."

"It's not my place."

Jason shook his head, disbelieving. "Indonesia. What the hell am I supposed to do there?"

"Indonesia?" That was what Luke had decided?

"The precious Maitland Foundation. I'm supposed to spend the next two years in hell."

"Beats jail," she said quietly.

"He couldn't prove it."

Not, I didn't do it. "It's not so bad. You might even like it. It might even be good for you."

"That's what he said." Jason strode away cursing, and Meg went back into the living room, resumed her seat on the couch. Such a world of difference between the two men. Outside, an engine roared into life. Tires screeched. Several minutes later Luke eased himself down beside her, slipped his arm back around her shoulders. He tugged her in close.

"Good choice." She chanced a glance at him. He didn't look happy but wasn't quite as grim as when he'd left.

He leaned closer, kissed the top of her head and for a second rested his cheek there. "I guess so. Now start this movie up again or I'll have to assume control of the remote." No mention of the fact that the roads must now be drivable.

Meg relaxed against him, breathed in his nearness and pressed the button for play.

If only.

If only they were a married couple and this was their life. If only he wanted to spend all his snowy afternoons, and rainy and sunny and windy ones, with her. A good man sharing the moments as he held her. Not to mention his nights and mornings, too. Instead of a man who wanted to have this brief time with her and then send her on her way.

Too soon the movie ended. She should stand, move away from Luke, get him to take her to Sally's. But she didn't move.

"The sequel's even better," he said, his arm still draped over her shoulders, his body pressed against hers.

"I'd heard that it was. So often they're not." She was pathetic. Wanting this. Wanting the crumbs of his presence and affection. She was too scared to analyze what it was she felt for her husband, but it was powerful enough that she wanted to eke out every moment she had left with him.

"I have it. Do you want to watch it?"

More than anything, because it bought her another couple of hours with Luke. She made to stand because another couple of hours only prolonged the inevitable. He wanted hours; she wanted years, a lifetime even. He pulled her effortlessly back down. "I should get going to Sally's," she said. She'd always been the type to rip a bandage off and get the pain over with.

"Should or want to?" He searched her face.

"Should." It was the last thing she wanted.

"Then don't. Stay here. This is okay, isn't it?" As though that was the only thing stopping her from staying.

This was so much better than okay, which was precisely why she *should* go to Sally's.

"I make a mean spaghetti Bolognese."

"Wouldn't it be better for both of us if I left now?"

He contemplated her question, gave it more thought

than she'd expected and she found herself on tenterhooks for his answer. Finally, he shook his head. "I like being near you, Meg. I don't know why. You ease something within me. I'm going to miss you when you go, so I'm in no hurry for that to happen."

He spoke an echo of her thoughts out loud.

Whatever time they had would be all that she would get. She wasn't going to curtail it. She sank back into the cushions of the couch, determined instead to make every minute, every second of these precious hours count, to store every moment in her memory.

As they watched the sequel, the afternoon bled into dusk which darkened quickly to night. They ate together, his spaghetti Bolognese as good as he'd claimed. And then they watched the third and final installment.

As the closing credits rolled, neither of them made any move to stand.

Far from it. "Lie down here with me," he said as though he knew that if she got up from the couch it would be to leave. It had to be. "It's wide enough."

So they lay down facing one another, heads on cushions. His hand resting at the curve of her waist.

"What will you do when you leave here?" he asked.

Meg chewed her lip. "Sally's offered me a job with the Maitland Foundation."

"You've accepted?"

She shook her head. "I wanted to see what you thought. Whether that might keep me too close?"

His hand curved more firmly around her. "The thought of having you close isn't such a terrible thing."

"But after people have thought we were married."

"We were married."

"Not properly."

He shifted his hand, found hers, touched a finger to the gold band adorning it. "Tell that to the minister."

"I just mean that it could be awkward."

"I do what I think is right. I thought, still do, that marrying you was the right thing to do at the time." He pulled her a little closer. "I've had no cause to regret that decision."

"You don't regret what we did last night?"

A smile spread across his face. "How could I possibly regret that? The very thought of it could sustain me for years to come."

"I can't help feeling that we're missing something. That we ought to be regretting it."

"In that case, you're thinking too much."

Maybe he was right. She was overthinking things. They'd had their night. She'd be able to take those memories and these with her, tucked up beside him, the scent of his cologne, the snow outside, the fire inside. He would be her benchmark, her standard. But he so far outshone anyone else she'd ever met that it was impossible to imagine that standard being reached again.

They lay on the couch talking for hours about everything and nothing. She'd never shared so much of herself with anyone or felt so honored and warmed by the trust he showed in sharing with her.

They changed positions so that he was spooned behind her, stroking her side. After a time his hand slowed and stopped. His breathing softened.

Meg still lay awake. "What if I loved you?" she whispered into the darkness.

She felt a deeper stillness steal over him.

He'd heard.

He said nothing.

And she knew there was no "what if" about it. Somewhere, somehow she'd fallen in love with him, with his quiet strength and his deep integrity, with his silver eyes and the way he kissed her, held her, and because he of all people seemed to see the person she was inside.

But he hadn't asked for that—her love.

"That wouldn't be a good idea," he said gently.

Luke felt Meg shrink a little away from him and against overriding impulse he didn't pull her back. She didn't really love him. She couldn't because he was all wrong for her. He was too old, too cynical about life and people and love. He was a loner. Wasn't he?

She deserved someone closer to her own age, someone closer to her in optimism and kindness. She imagined qualities in him he didn't have.

He would let her go. Set her free.

In the morning.

And the thought filled him with desolation. It was the thought of a Meg-less existence that broke his resolve, made him pull her in closer to him, made him try to absorb a little of her essence into himself. He wanted something from her that he'd never wanted from a woman before—just to be with her, to have her near. And the nearer the better. The feelings were so new that he didn't know what to do with them, how to deal with them.

She'd helped him so much. Helped him on the island when he'd first been injured, helped him by marrying him, and the very thought of her had sustained him when he'd been ill. Even now, lying here like this, her breathing soft and gentle, she soothed something within him, filled and completed him. In so many ways she was his better half. But she deserved more. She deserved to find her own better half.

So he would help her by letting her go.

* * *

The doorbell chimed through the house. Meg and Luke struggled to sitting, his arm falling from her. Through the windows a clear, bright day showed snow-covered mountains on the far side of the crystalline lake. Meg had never been so disappointed to see a beautiful day.

Luke stood, running a hand through his hair as he looked down at her. "That'll be Mark."

His attorney. That announcement, more than the weather even, told her that her time with Luke was over. She'd served her purpose, and in return had found a deep, brief perfection. That would be enough. It had to be.

They walked to the front door together. He would take Mark to his office. "This shouldn't take too long."

She nodded. She'd be gone before then. It was the best, the only, way. She wasn't going to stay for the humiliation of the terms he wanted to end their connection with, no matter how gently he would do it.

He turned for his office. Mark looked at her, pity in his gaze. "He'll look after you," he murmured.

Great, even his attorney felt sorry for her.

Luke stopped at the office door. "Wait," he said as though he knew she'd already decided to go. He held her gaze until she nodded.

Unable to stay in the house where for such a brief time she'd found bliss, Meg took Caesar outside, striding unseeing along the path she'd walked so often, and tried to shut out her awareness of the ticking time bomb that was Luke's meeting with Mark.

Caesar found and then dropped a stick in the center of the path. "Not today, buddy." She strode past it, but when he next overtook her, it was back in his mouth.

It was over. Her fantasy. And she knew the answer to

the question she'd posed to Luke—would her working close by be a problem. It might not be for him, but it would be for her. Seeing him and having to not let him see she loved him. Hearing people talk about him. Seeing him dating other women. No, it definitely wasn't going to work for her. She wasn't that reasonable. She wasn't that thick-skinned.

She stopped at the base of a dead and blackened pine that alone had at some point been struck by lightning. Caesar dropped his stick and sniffed, his nose tracking to the body of a small bird, a mountain chickadee, lying still and stiff. Meg stared at the little corpse, her heart breaking at the sight.

She had to leave.

Despite tacitly agreeing to wait, she couldn't. She would get her car and go. She would do it before the meeting was even over, before Luke and Mark gently, kindly explained the details of how her happiness was to end. Because she knew she couldn't take their explanations with anything like the dignity they deserved. She considered her options. Sally would come if she called. Her friend would take her to collect her car. And then she could go. Somewhere. Anywhere. Away.

Pulling her phone from her pocket, she hurried back along the path. She caught sight of the lake and the snow-capped mountains through the screen of pine trees and stopped. It was a sight that had always filled her with peace and given her strength. She took a moment to absorb the view for the last time.

Caesar dropped his stick onto her foot.

She shook her head at him. "You don't give up, do you, buddy?" She bent to pick up the stick and stilled with her fingers wrapped around its roughened bark.

He didn't give up. He *never* gave up. Not when it came

to something he wanted. Even now he watched her, tail wagging, willing her to throw the stick.

Crystal-clear understanding and resolution welled within her.

Meg straightened and threw the stick. She wasn't running away. Not this time. She wasn't subjugating her needs. She wasn't going to go without telling Luke that she loved him. Without asking him to at least try to love her back. To give her, them, a chance.

Something had begun between them back on the island and that something had blossomed and grown into so much more.

He'd said himself that she should give her needs priority, ask more for the things she wanted. And the only thing, the only one, she wanted and needed was him.

He could grow to love her back. She knew it. He just had to let himself. Because not only was he necessary to her, she was, if not necessary, then at least good, for him. She believed that much with all her heavy heart. A heart that nurtured an insistent flicker of hope.

All she had to lose was her pride. And it was worth the sacrifice to know that she wasn't going to turn tail. She ran. Not away from him but toward him, toward their home, up the steps pausing briefly at the Christmas tree to make her wish on the single bright star at its top and burst into his office.

Conversation stopped as Luke and Mark looked up at her from the leather armchairs in front of Luke's desk, surprise in two pairs of eyes. They both stood. Meg's gaze went briefly to the single thin stack of papers neatly aligned on Luke's desk. Divorce papers? Her heart hammered in her chest.

She walked up to Luke, lifted the mistletoe she'd

pulled from the Christmas tree and held it above his head. Stretching up onto her tiptoes, she kissed him, joining her mouth to his, trying to put a forewarning of her love into the tenderness of her kiss.

His arms slid obligingly around her waist, he angled his head to deepen the kiss. She could almost give in to the temptation of just this, being held in his arms. But she needed more. She broke the kiss, stepped back and out of his hold. "Mark, I want to talk to my husband. Alone." She kept her gaze on Luke, he met it steadily, emotions in his eyes she didn't dare interpret and a glimmer of wry amusement at her demand.

"I was just going. I'll see myself out." Mark's voice reached her seconds before he shut the office door quietly behind him. Leaving her alone with Luke.

For the longest time she stared at him, he was everything to her; he was the man she loved. She just had to tell him that.

She took a deep breath and pointed to his desk. "I won't sign those papers."

He frowned and his gaze flicked to the desk.

"I don't care what you're offering. I want more. I want you. I'm not going to let you shut me out of your life because you don't want to need anyone. It doesn't work that way. You need me. You just don't know it. And I...I need you. I love you. You might not be ready for that yet, but you have to give it, me, a chance."

Luke closed the distance she'd tried to establish and pressed a finger to her lips, silencing her. He eased the mistletoe from her fingers, held it above her head and sliding his finger from her lips, replaced it with his mouth, looped his arms once more around her.

Too soon he broke the kiss. "I don't want you to sign those papers."

"You don't?"

"No." He shook his head and a smile touched his lips. "They're to do with Jason. Not you. Not us."

"But I thought...Mark...he wasn't here because of me, because of you wanting a divorce?"

"We did discuss you."

"And?"

"I told him we'd slept together."

"And?"

"And I told him I love you, which was wrong of me."

Because it wasn't the truth? Her jaw clenched with the force of suppressed emotion.

He stroked his thumbs over her cheeks. "Because you should have been the first one I told." He brushed a kiss across her lips. "It wasn't until Mark walked in that I was forced to contemplate a Meg-less existence. The prospect was dreadful. From the first moment I saw you, I knew you were somehow necessary to me. I didn't realize how or why, but I do now. I want you in my life, my home, my heart. Always. If you'll have me."

Meg nodded, her throat too clogged to speak.

"Is that a yes?"

She nodded again.

He lifted his hands to her face, his silver eyes glittering with emotion. "Hi, honey, we're home," he said. And then, finally, he kissed her.

* * * * *

Silhouette Desire

COMING NEXT MONTH

Available January 11, 2011

HARLEQUIN®

A *Romance*

FOR EVERY MOOD™

Spotlight on

Classic

Quintessential, modern love stories
that are romance at its finest.

See the next page
to enjoy a sneak peek from
the Harlequin Presents® series.

*Harlequin Presents® is thrilled
to introduce the first installment of
an epic tale of passion and drama by*
USA TODAY *Bestselling Author*
Penny Jordan!

**When buttoned-up Giselle first meets
the devastatingly handsome Saul Parenti,
the heat between them is explosive....**

"LET ME GET THIS STRAIGHT. Are you actually suggesting that I would stoop to that kind of game playing?"

Saul came out from behind his desk and walked toward her. Giselle could smell his hot male scent and it was making her dizzy, igniting a low, dull, pulsing ache that was taking over her whole body.

Giselle defended her suspicions. "You don't want me here."

"No," Saul agreed, "I don't."

And then he did what he had sworn he would not do, cursing himself beneath his breath as he reached for her, pulling her fiercely into his arms and kissing her with all the pent-up fury she had aroused in him from the moment he had first seen her.

Giselle certainly *wanted* to resist him. But the hand she raised to push him away developed a will of its own and was sliding along his bare arm beneath the sleeve of his shirt, and the body that should have been arching away from him was instead melting into him.

Beneath the pressure of his kiss he could feel and taste her gasp of undeniable response to him. He wanted to devour her, take her and drive them both until they were equally satiated—even whilst the anger within him that she should make him feel that way roared and burned its resentment of his need.

She was helpless, Giselle recognized, totally unable to withstand the storm lashing at her, able only to cling to the man who was the cause of it and pray that she would survive.

Somewhere else in the building a door banged. The sound exploded into the sensual tension that had enclosed them, driving them apart. Saul's chest was rising and falling as he fought for control; Giselle's whole body was trembling.

Without a word she turned and ran.

Find out what happens when Saul and Giselle succumb to their irresistible desire in

THE RELUCTANT SURRENDER

Available January 2011 from Harlequin Presents®

HPEXP0111

Silhouette *Desire*

HAVE BABY,
NEED BILLIONAIRE

MAUREEN CHILD

Simon Bradley is accomplished, successful
and very proud. The fact that he has to
prove he's fit to be a father to his own child
is preposterous. Especially when he has to
prove it to Tula Barrons, one of the most
scatterbrained women he's ever met. But Simon
has a ruthless plan to win Tula over and when
passion overrules prudence one night, it opens
up the door to an affair that leaves them both
staggering. Will this billionaire bachelor learn
to love more than his fortune?

*Billionaires
and Babies*

*Available January
wherever books are sold.*

Always Powerful, Passionate and Provocative.